YOU,
BLEEDING CHILDHOOD

You, Bleeding Childhood

MICHELE MARI

Translated from the Italian
by Brian Robert Moore

SHEFFIELD – LONDON – NEW YORK

Originally published as *Tu, sanguinosa infanzia*

First edition in English published in 2023 by And Other Stories
Sheffield – London – New York
www.andotherstories.org

Copyright © 2009 and 2018 Giulio Einaudi editore s.p.a., Torino

"The Soccer Balls of Mr. Kurz" and "Eurydice Had a Dog" originally published
in *Euridice aveva un cane* © 2004 and 2015 Giulio Einaudi editore s.p.a., Torino

Translation copyright © 2023 Brian Robert Moore
Translator's afterword copyright © 2023 Brian Robert Moore

1 3 5 7 9 8 6 4 2

ISBN: 9781913505684
eBook ISBN: 9781913505691

Editor: Jeremy M. Davies; Copy-editor: Gesche Ipsen; Proofreader:
Sarah Terry; Cover design: Holly Ovenden; Typeset in Albertan Pro and Syntax
by Tetragon, London. Printed and bound by CPI Limited, Croydon, UK.

And Other Stories gratefully acknowledge that our work is
supported using public funding by Arts Council England.

This book is a co-production with the Italian Cultural Institute in
London and was made possible by a special funding of the Italian
Ministry of Foreign Affairs and International Cooperation

Supported using public funding by
**ARTS COUNCIL
ENGLAND**

MIX
Paper | Supporting
responsible forestry
FSC www.fsc.org **FSC® C171272**

ISTITUTO
italiano
DI CULTURA
LONDRA

Ministry of Foreign Affairs
and International Cooperation

CONTENTS

from *Eurydice Had a Dog*

COMIC STRIPS

When he learned that he was going to become a father, Professor —— shut himself for a long while in his study to get his thoughts in order. In the midst of so many looming uncertainties, he came out of that room with one thing certain: the comics, the dear comic strips from his childhood had to be stored away for safekeeping.

For thirty years that beloved bundle of treasures had occupied one of the highest shelves of his vast library, a position that, while banishing those pages to the unreachable heights of the science fiction series Urania and the tales of monsters, nevertheless exalted them to an eminence before which all the other books—the "real" books, the "serious" books—had to bow down. The professor knew, of course, that the nobility of his library resided in the products of sixteenth-century printing presses and in his baroque folios, in the volumes of Antonio Zatta's *Parnaso* and in the beauty of his Bodonis, that its academic pinnacles found name and substance in critical and national editions; he had known for some time that this immense family had grown with the Silvestri and Sonzogno imprints, the Medusa and Struzzi series, and that it had been refined by the Oxford blues and the brick-yellow of his Belles Lettres, by the human abundance of the Pléiade and Ricciardi collections, and by the defunct rigor of the

Lerici catalogue. But he knew, too, that without that initial foundation his library—and therefore his life—would have been like a great fruit with no stalk; as if, plucked from that original life-giving tree, all those learned writings would have been destined to shrivel up and wither away. Pascoli and his poetics of the inner child had nothing to do with it, the professor irritably declared to himself, it was rather a question of proper sequence, of material justification: you won't be the owner of a bed if you have never slept in a crib, if you haven't been rocked in a cradle. Similarly, you won't absorb Columella or Malebranche if you haven't absorbed Collodi's *Pinocchio* or Salgari's pirates. In his house in the country, he still had all of his old childhood beds, lined up in the same room like an allegory of the ages of man—and should he not have conserved as sacred the first works he'd read? Were they not perhaps a document—proof!—of his childhood and, at the same time, of his anguished struggle to never leave that childhood behind, while the world, seemingly out for blood, had been plotting all along to tear it away from him, bludgeoning him with fears, with horrendous itches, with ambiguous intellectual conquests (*The Epic Reawakening! The Way of Man!*), blindly doling out blows? Deeply, he felt that if life is corruption and abjuration, then it must be highly moral to counter its general ruin with the opposing process of redemption, of affectionate disinterment.

And so it had been with those comic books of his, jealously safeguarded as his most valuable possessions. How many times, upon hearing someone his age express perplexed ignorance over the fate of their old comics, had he felt an invaluable sense of triumph and reward for not having squandered, for not having caved—like the others—to the humiliating blackmail of growing up at the cost of betrayal!

Now, though, a baby was on the way. High up there, his comics would be out of reach and even out of sight for the future critter; but, even so, a few feminine words had been enough to alarm him: "Just think, someday your old comics will be good for Filippuccio." *Will* be good? They had been, they were good—he would have liked to protest—retaining their goodness like an everlasting luminescence. But he did not speak, for right away he had to obey an even stronger impulse to climb up there and retrieve them, those blessed things so unexpectedly ensnared. After redescending with the entire stack, he blew on them to remove the majority of the dust; then he undid the twine that bound them together, and once again the relics spread out before his emotional eyes.

He considered them closely. Every *Tintin*; each of the original editions of *Cocco Bill*; countless issues of *The Phantom*, just a couple of issues of *Mandrake the Magician*; a few issues of *Nembo Kid*, a few of *Jeff Hawke*, the first three years of *Linus*, that first *Mickeyneid*, that first *Donaldduckyssey*, two issues of *Creepy*, and still more, still a few more loosed relics. As always happened on such occasions, an imperceptible pause spent lingering on a given cover was all it took for him to succumb to the urge to pick the book up; and having picked it up, to start to reread; and having started to reread, to devour it from cover to cover. In this manner he reread *Cigars of the Pharaoh*, then *The Cossack Cocco Bill*, then *The Seven Crystal Balls*; after which—more than two hours had passed—he shook himself back to life with a doleful shudder, heaved a deep sigh, and spoke to himself as follows: "These are a crystallization of my dreams, the only not-sad glimmer in my life; they are documents, fossils of an age that entreats me to pay it homage; they are little cadavers that refuse to die; they are such that *I alone* know what they are. And all this should be 'used'? It should go back to being something 'current,' tomorrow? Current! These monstrous coagulations, these superhuman concentrations of my melancholy, these monuments of my solitude, these SACRED things are to end up in the hands of a little critter (loved, no doubt—my own flesh and blood, even), a *slobbering* critter who will scribble on them with obscene crayons, with even more obscene *pens*? They are imbued with my own sequels and re-elaborations, entities such as these, they compartmentalize unrepeatable days, such vignettes (beloved squares, adored rectangles, emblems of my room, insignias of my bed), yes, yes, they are *history*, musealized and annotated *laudatissima historia*, they are a *docta collectio* (codified, catalogued) meriting scientific discipline, distance, the love owed to the classics (Tacitus, Proust, Guicciardini—Soldino, Geppo, Eega Beeva), and they are, and they are tradition, and they are religion. And they are emotion. Enough. I handle them with care, *I* who possessed them, touching them with imaginary gloves, turning their pages with mental tweezers as if they were invaluable papyruses—*I* who was their master—and now others are to establish with them a *practical* relationship of immediate gratification, reify them in such a way? No, it's too late for that. One can no longer have fun with what is cloaked in an aura, one cannot carnally commingle with our object of worship, nor put it under examination when there is only room left for contemplation. Forgive me, future Filippuccio, but if, among your future comics (you, homologous to them, and they, organic to you), I were to slip in these ancient ones of mine, you would not recognize the categorial difference, the inherent transcendency, the axiological superiority; approaching one of them—this wondrous *Cocco Bill in Canada*, for example—you wouldn't whisper to yourself, 'Behold, *that* comic has at last come back to us!' (and has returned *thus*, unchanged and perfect), you wouldn't predispose your whole being to taking a gluttonous and at the same time painful gulp, no: you would say, brutally, 'Huh, a comic, let's see what it's about, let's see if it tickles our fancy.' But the holy scriptures, Filippo, do not tolerate the criticism of modern men, nor indeed will it be tolerated by me, their priest. Not only doodles and tears, Filippo, are blasphemous affronts, so, too, is indifference, the glance that clumps together and knows no hierarchy, the adiaphorous passivity of the profaner. I close my eyes and I see you, quick little ghost, looking, rummaging, finding, flipping through the pages, I see you toss this worn *Phantom* into a corner after just a couple of pages—you, fruit of my loins, not falling madly in love with the Phantom! I saw you: you gave a huff, you weren't impressed! You seek comfort—and find it—in other books that mean nothing to me, stuff that is yours and yours alone, and so I hereby officially allot them to you, let those be your dreams, and if from that jumble you're one day able to extract the gold that I've extracted from my comics, then my compliments to you: life always starts from scratch, it's not as though you'd want to inherit Daddy's emotions, Daddy's memories, Daddy's consciousness, and just insert

13

it all into your little brain like a transplant, would you? So go ahead and get started, for I'm wrapping up, I'll now take what's necessary and pack it away, burying it in the basement, shielding it from the contamination of your impish spirit (to not love the black grilles of Tintin's cars! to be hard-hearted before the power of kryptonite! forever blind to the dialectic that sparkles between Dick Tracy and Fearless Fosdick!), you won't even know that my comics all lie in this trunk, you won't even be able to look for them, never shall I hear you ask me to show them to you for just a second . . . 'a second'! Like liquidating an entire civilization with a single glance! I *am* the cowboy Cocco Bill, understand? So if you don't dedicate your childhood to Cocco Bill—and you certainly won't—then it will be as though you renounced your father, as though at the dinner table one evening you were to turn to your mother and, pointing with your pudding-smeared spoon, ask her, 'Mommy, who's this man eating with us?' Cocco Bill is who I am! Captain Haddock is who I am! Wellington Wimpy! Ellsworth! Brainiac! Is that enough for you? That halfwit Jimmy Olsen, yes, him too! This is your father! Answer me one question: Chamomile tea—who consumed it? What about mountains of hamburgers? Or—need I even ask—kumquats? But you don't know anything, not a thing. What do you know about issue no. 7 of the comic supplement of *Il Giorno*, that little booklet published in the first few days of July 1962? It was titled *Kamumilla Kokobì*, and now I've said everything that needs to be said. *Kamumilla Kokobì* . . . Something more or less like the *Iliad* . . . Ah, enough, enough, it hurts too much to talk about these things—comic strips, what comic strips? You're not even born yet and your father is bringing all this to a close, *finis*, the topic's exhausted, to be all aflutter in such a manner is simply not okay, end of discussion; one grows up alone, lives alone, dies alone, we'll try to meet each other on other planes, we'll play chess, go to the movies together, I'll teach you to use Vinavil glue, someday I'll give you a book by Stevenson as a present. But these comics, Filippo, cannot be shared, they are the flower of my childhood, you see, and they are, therefore, my essence: if you take them away from me, you kill me; take away the *Divine Comedy*, take away *Moby-Dick*, even take away Aulus Gellius, all of the Loeb Library—you want the Battaglia too? You want *Rerum Italicarum scriptores*, the Ramusio? But don't ask for *Kamumilla Kokobì*, don't ever ask for it, don't ever so much as smile at the holy names, I'll snuff out that smile here and now by hiding my treasure, for you'll admit that if I didn't, I'd be forced to live out the humiliation of subterfuge, think long and hard about that humiliation, a university professor who locks himself in the bathroom to reread a *Tintin* without his son knowing! And in my study, too, I would hide—'Daddy, what are you doing?' 'I'm working on the critical edition of Castiglione's Latin eclogues, off you go, I need to concentrate.' But no, Daddy's brain is jerking off to Jeff Hawke's metallic beetles, if you stretch your neck you'll see the pages of *Jeff Hawke* poking out of the eclogues, no, please don't condemn me to all that, one day if you like I'll give you a seven-hour lesson on jerking off but that's enough for now, let me close the book on all this, if you can see me from the *antemundia* where you currently dwell, then look, look, I'm closing the book, you see? Book closed."

THE MAN WHO SHOT
LIBERTY VALANCE

He wore an embarrassed smile, my father, while looking me in the eyes in my dream last night. There was a door next to us, and when he asked me if I knew what was on the other side of it, I simply replied that I did not want to go in.

"I didn't ask you if you want to go through the door, but if you know what's on the other side."

"It's for the best if I never find out, Dad. If it's something unknown, it will be horrific; if it's something familiar, it will be sad."

But you kept on insisting, and when your look softened, began to gleam with that special light that recognizes me as the same as you, all of my defenses left me.

Now that the dream is over, I wonder why you didn't actually do it—this thing, which, if I was able to dream it up last night, you surely must have imagined for yourself—why you didn't dare do it while there was still time. This void that echoes inside me, this grief that day after day has saddened the days of my life, now I know where it all comes from; now I know where the most secret part of my soul has fled whenever the vile world has tried to tear me to bits.

*

"Do you recognize it?" My father was showing me a fifty-centimeter Winchester rifle. "Purchased on December 20, 1963, in a store in Corso Vercelli; given on December 25, 1963, with the following card: 'To Mike, for saving my life— Johnny Guitar'; used without interruption from December 25, 1963 until May 9, 1964."

"What . . . what happened on May 9?"

"You lost it. It slipped through the slats of a bench in Piazza Napoli, and when your grandfather stood up to go back home, you followed him without a moment's hesitation."

"Really? Just like that? That's how it happened?"

"Just like that. And these, do you recognize these?" In the palm of his right hand were three Mercury toy cars, four and a half centimeters long, made of bulky enameled iron: a yellow one, a red one, a green one. I reached out to take them, but my father closed his fist. "Purchased on December 18, 1964, in a store in Via Foppa by your father on behalf of your grandparents; given on December 25, 1964, with no accompanying written material; used without interruption from December 26, 1964 until February 19, 1968, the day of a deplorable trade with a classmate, which you certainly ought to remember."

Did I ever! His name was Federico Colla, he was a year older than me, and one cursed day he offered me a plastic box containing tiddlywinks and pick-up sticks. He offered them to me *in exchange*—yes, he committed this act of violence against me—and I was depraved enough to accept. His plastic in exchange for my iron! But . . .

"But I only gave him two cars, because I'd already lost the yellow one down a storm drain not long before . . . "

"Oh, and you think that changes things, do you?"

17

"No, Dad, it doesn't change a thing."

"Correct. It doesn't. In any case, you would have regretted the trade immediately even if you'd only let him have a single wheel—because it was a Mercury wheel, and it was *your* wheel."

"Mine, yes—it was mine."

"Don't get too emotional, son, because we've only just begun. Otherwise, how will you be able to handle seeing things like this—" (in his arms there had appeared a little fortress made of bamboo) "—or this—" (the No. 5 Meccano set) "—or this—" (*The Adventures of Saturnin Farandoul*, half its pages detached from the spine) "or this, or this, or this—"

"Stop, I'm begging you, have mercy!"

"*Saturnin Farandoul*, how you loved that book! But that didn't stop you, one day, from letting someone get between Saturnin and you. An overeager grandfather who politely asked you—because he *did* ask you—if the book could be passed down to a younger cousin, seeing as you—"

"Don't say iiit!"

"Seeing as you were now a 'big boy' . . . Do you want the date, the exact date of your betrayal?"

"That cousin, how I hated him for it!"

"Of course you did. And who can say whether, after him, there wasn't an even younger recipient, or whether he held on to Saturnin forever, or if one day he threw that old book into the trash—who knows?"

"But it's here, you just showed it to me."

"And these marbles, what do you have to say about them? They didn't require too much space at the end of the day, just a little sack in the corner of your drawer. And yet, at a certain point, game over: they wound up being expelled from your life."

"That's a lie! It's the things themselves that disappear. I would have given my own life for those marbles, how could I have abandoned them? My marbles . . . "

"There you have it, *they disappear.* The trick is never to become distracted, never let your guard down . . . to know at all times *what* one has and *where* one has it . . . and, after you've loved something for even a single morning, to keep it close until the day you die. To keep, to keep, to keep . . ."

"Never regretting the loss of a single thing . . ."

"This model fortress, for example. One day you forgot you had it, and you never gave it another thought. But on the inside, from that day on, you missed it—missed it when you looked at that special girl in your high school class, or when you studied Thomas Hobbes, or when you polished your bicycle. You missed it the day you got married, when Berlinguer died, every time you took the number twenty-nine tram—always and everywhere, you still missed it. Even yesterday morning, from the beginning to the end of your faculty meeting, you went on missing it."

"It's true, Dad, because we made it together with Vinavil glue, and it's so imbued with our essence that it seems almost obscene to me now, this fortress, I can barely even look at it. You were wearing a white shirt with ink-stained cuffs, and I was wearing a burgundy sweater, and you were singing to yourself, '*Besciamboeu, the cow and the bull.*' Oh Dad, how is it possible that one day I simply stopped thinking about it? I, who for my entire life have been a morbid, fetishistic keeper of everything that was mine, archiving it all with obsessive

19

affection, how could *I* have possibly committed so many acts of betrayal?"

"You see, Michele, one can never be too morbidly attached, because as much as one might live off the past, there's always going to be something in the present, unavoidably, to coerce and humiliate us. Distractions, compulsions, good excuses to throw off a few blankets and let some fresh air into the stuffiness of which your life has consisted—so long, consistency! New schools, new houses, new lights, and in the meantime we've prostituted ourselves to just about anybody and anything, to the point that we've actually lost ourselves . . . But all it takes is for a picture from back when we were seven or ten years old to fall into our hands, and we melt with emotion like wandering adventurers laying their eyes once again on their homeland: 'There,' we shout, 'that's what I am, no doubt about it, I'm still the same!' But, in the meantime, you have squandered. If you have twenty toys and you hold on to eighteen, you're already toast. A certain pocketknife with a mother-of-pearl handle, a single red enamel magnet, as soon as you push them aside, however lightheartedly ('Stay here for a bit,' you say affectionately, as you tuck them away in a drawer), that's it, you're toast. You've become a squanderer."

"You don't have to tell me these things, Dad. I know them better than you do."

"In fact, it wasn't my intention. I only wanted to give you a present."

My father looked tired now, perhaps because of the look of uncertainty roving in his eyes. I was trying not to stare at the heaps of objects surrounding us.

"I'd watch you," he said, "after you lost or traded something, and I'd feel so bad for you—such a restless little creature, pacing up and down the hallway with a face like someone who'd had his soul ripped out, someone who *just couldn't understand.* So one day I made up my mind, and became your custodian angel. I went to the little park in Piazza Napoli, and the Johnny Guitar rifle was still there, hidden in the grass; I snuck into Mr. and Mrs. Colla's apartment while they were watching TV, slipped into their sleeping son's bedroom, and retrieved the Mercury cars; I went to your cousin's cousin's house, and I confiscated Saturnin Farandoul. Wherever the diaspora had reached, I went: amid so many unfamiliar items, your things shone with the love that had been in your eyes—I couldn't miss them. 'This is Michelino's, don't mind me!'—and from the heap I'd pick out the single marble that had been yours, unstick from an album of trading cards the one soccer player who had been squeezed between your fingertips. Then, inevitably, I even developed the habit of recovering your belongings that were still in our home but had been left to gather dust. After a whole year of disuse, that mother-of-pearl knife and that scarlet magnet could have been considered, to all intents and purposes, lost—and that's when I'd step in."

"And you think I didn't realize that after a little while certain things of mine could no longer be found where they were supposed to be? All my useless searching, and the thief was you! But I've never loved you as much as I do now that you've told me."

"Don't get too misty-eyed, because you're about to see something that will blow right through your heart."

And then I saw once again the love of all loves: my teddy bear, the agonizing entity that corresponded to the *flatus vocis* of "teddy," my bear of ripped and faded gray cloth, tarnished, blinded, piss-stained, flattened.

"Purchased—"

"Give it to me!"

"You're almost forty years old, you can't act like a little kid anymore. As I was saying: purchased on September 29, 1958, at the department store La Rinascente, given the same day and used without interruption from then until December 26, 1968. And without interruption, this time, truly means without interruption."

"The interruption . . . was you?"

"You turned thirteen years old that day. If I hadn't taken it away from you, you would be sleeping with it even now. It was the only instance in which I allowed myself to lay hands on something you still kept by your side. At dawn, I tiptoed into the room where you were sleeping, and I slipped it out from under your arms."

"You decided to play the pedagogue! You were impatient to see me grow up! What a wonderful, caring angel! Stealing things from me as if I were just another Federico Colla!"

"Think about it: you were literally eating away at this bear, it was becoming embedded between your ribs, seeping slowly but surely into your bloodstream. But now, instead, you have it here, whole, like your other toys."

"Sure, let's put it that way—but really it's mortifying to put it that way. And, in fact, I'm not going to put it any way at all! And don't call it a toy! Look at me, look at this wretched son of yours, look at how he had to live from that day on, as though he were already at death's door. At thirteen I became a dead man walking. And you want to give it back to me *now*? For twenty-seven years you kept it in your studio, twenty-seven years of *my* life! The greasy marble that was handsome little Michelino's! The rifle that goes *ping*. 'Oh my heart, oh let us embrace, Father!' That's the kind of touching finale you were expecting, eh? A syrupy melting of our chromosomes? Absolutely not! This finale is poison, life is horrific, if God is in bears then why are we men so interested in pussy? You realize that at the age of fifteen I read all of Plutarch just to fill the void that was left? That my whole life long I've dreamed of slaughtering a dozen people a day, that today my diet consists principally of benzodiazepine? That there isn't enough water in the world to quench the burning thirst inside me?"

"Would you prefer to talk about Lemmy Caution? About Liberty Valance?"

"Yes, let's talk about Liberty Valance—about the man who shot Liberty Valance."

THE COVERS OF URANIA

Maybe the sweetest dream I ever had was when Robert Louis Stevenson came to ask me if I would lend him a few of my Urania paperbacks. "I should ask my grandpa first. They were his," I replied, but already his long fingers were caressing no. 17; already, I knew that book would end up in Polynesia. And he said, "Your grandpa is fine with it, I already checked with him myself." And never in my life have I felt so touched by grace.

Fact sheet. Urania is launched on October 10, 1952 with *The Sands of Mars* by Arthur C. Clarke (trans. Maria Gallone); the cover—on which the title of the series, THE NOVELS OF URANIA, is printed enclosed in a little box—is by Ć. Ćaesar, who is replaced by Carlo Jacono in 1957. In 1958, the branding also changes (URANIA: THE MOST FAMOUS SCIENCE-FICTION SERIES), as does the color of the spine (from white to red). In 1960, the first cover by Karel Thole appears; he will go on to provide cover art for over thirty years (with rare incursions by Ferenc Pinter). In 1962 (January), the trim size is reduced from 20 x 13.7 cm to 18.9 x 12.9 cm and (in May) the spine reverts to white (with the exception of a variously colored rectangle at the bottom): concurrently, the series branding begins to be printed inside a diamond, which shares the color of the spinal rectangle. In 1964, the cover art, previously quadrangular, becomes round (with a red border); the rectangle disappears from the spine. 1967 sees the end of the diamond; freed from any geometric shape, the branding is condensed to read, simply, URANIA; a red line separates the series name from the cover art: Urania persists in this incarnation to this day (1995).

Therefore, in order of increasing value and aura: "the rounds," "the rounds with the diamond," "the diamonds," "the little reds," "the big reds," "the old whites," "issue no. 1" [continued].

The little boy who still doesn't know how to read sees those thin books in his grandfather's hands (that uninterrupted *series* of books) and infers his own notion of peril: sensing in his elder a shaman, and in the books an initiatory *clavis* to horrific yet solemn Mysteries. If he can handle all of those illustrated monsters and live to tell the tale—this is the boy's little brain's awestruck discovery—then he must have entered into an agreement with them (making agreements with Monsters!), poor Grandpa, tremendous Grandpa, condemned to never slip up, the slightest error and the Monsters will be merciless with him, with Grandma, with the grandson who spends every Sunday at their house, all of them gobbled up in one go, an immediate mangling. And so the little boy examines him from afar, watches while his grandfather reads one of those books, pretending to play one of his games but in fact fulfilling the role of witness that has fallen to him: poor Grandpa, what torments is he suffering for our sake—is everything okay there, Grandpa? Is your reading *working out*?

And, creeping undetected until he's just a few steps away, the boy cranes his neck to peek once again at those nightmare forms, thinking that Grandpa is in their presence, he seems to be sitting here but he's actually with them, in who knows what obscure point of the infinite universe.

Editors: 1952 G. Monicelli, 1962 C. Fruttero, 1964 C. Fruttero and F. Lucentini, 1981 G. Montanari, 1990 G. Lippi.

Publishing directors: 1952 G. Marchiori, 1961 E. Pagliara, 1966 A. Tedeschi, 1979 A. Polillo, 1984 L. Grimaldi, 1990 G. Orsi.

Price: 150 lire in 1952, 200 in 1963, 250 in 1967, 300 in 1970, 350 in 1972, 400 in 1974, 500 in 1975, 600 in 1976, 700 in 1977 (text omitted) [continued].

Those Urania covers . . . first and foremost: monsters upon monsters, of every type and form: loricate and scaly, cataphracted, furry, slobbery, slimy, flaming, ungulate, bituminous, lobated, crested, gaseous, glutinous, shapeless and misshapen, heraldic, enormous, abominable, solitary, flocked, frenzied, infiltrating, prognathous, chthonic, zoomorphic, cachinnatious, metaphysical, mucoidal, ulcerated, petrosal, gnarly, fibrous, exploded, amoebic, crepuscular, darting, ancient, putrid, rutilant, majestic, filamentous, vermiform, sentient, horrifying, always horrifying, yes, figures of plastic horror throbbing to *come out of those covers*, how not to feel it, how not to sense that those ghastly mouths were hankering for you, that those mutilated eyeballs were staring at you, and that if you weren't quick in putting the book back on the shelf, that dripping runoff would absorb you forever.

When there weren't monsters, there were vestiges or theaters of unspeakable horrors: scattered boneyards, deserted realms under copper skies, blood-red planets, wreckage and rubble, tuffaceous karsts, the semblances of condensed screams, *lacrimae rerum* of the cosmos. Then, sublimating and veering toward abstraction: strange prisms, spheres, cubes, spirals, vortexes, perspective distortions, labyrinths, oxymorons, anachronisms, hybridisms, metamorphisms, dadaisms, surrealisms, oneirisms.

Always and everywhere, the iconography of anguish.

The "Variety" section: From its outset, the series offers an ample appendix of short stories, scientific curiosities, and vignettes at the end of each volume. The comic strip *B.C.* (by J. Hart) appears regularly from 1962 onward, along with, from 1966, *The Wizard of Id* (by J. Hart and B. Parker).

Interior illustrations: Anonymous, in black and white (often mere section-break decorations: a tiny comet or rocket); they don't last beyond 1962 [continued].

The child, who by now knows how to read, takes a volume off the shelf and, without looking, immediately opens it at the back and searches for *B.C.* and *The Wizard*: he knows that these are akin to his daily bread, that if subjected to questioning by adults it will be considered a permissible helping, and that it is in his best interest not to stray beyond the limits of these comic strips. But before he can put the volume back to take another, forewarned by a restlessness in his fingertips, it inevitably slips through his hands: flipped like an omelet, the Urania reveals its face, that terrifying cover which, lurking behind the comic strips, was from the beginning the consciously desired object of his distressed sampling.

> Reprints: The best books begin to be reprinted in 1963, repaginated and with new covers; numerous are the instances in which Thole, without outlandish variations, reillustrates his own covers.

> Translators: Among the multitude, it is worth memorializing here the two women who, put together, translated roughly half of the entire series: Hilja Brinis and Beata Della Frattina [continued].

Grandfather's Uranias were for me the dark side of literature. In those thin little volumes that simultaneously attracted and repelled me, my tremulous spirit found all the obscene excess it couldn't find in other books. I thus convinced myself, when I was around eight years old, that *The Little Prince* or *The Jungle Book* were the first steps in a long initiation process that would one day allow me, after decades and decades of reading, to finally be able to read, like my grandfather, Robert Heinlein's *The Terrors of the Sixth Moon*.* And such names as Heinlein, Sheckley, Clarke, Simak, Wyndham, Matheson, Silverberg, Pohl, and Van Vogt made up for me the supreme canon of Western literature, a constellation of superior spirits elected by the monsters to reveal to us humans the

---

* Note from the translator: The book titles used in this story correspond to the Italian titles that appear on the Urania covers. When a book's Italian title differs markedly from the English original, a translation of the Italian title has been used. A list of the original titles of the principal books referenced can be found in the "Title translations" section on p. 35.

monstrous laws of the universe: and while admiring them, I questioned only whether they were still people at all, or whether, elevated to such extreme limits of consciousness, they themselves—in their very limbs—did not instead make up a part of that monstrousness. "Wyndham, Wyndham," I whispered, and the sound seemed a wind blowing from a dead city; "Simak, Simak," and I heard the clacking of giant claws; "Pohl," and there was a bubble, a single bubble, emerging from the slimy lake in which skulked, unseen, the Beast.

External advertisements: The back covers are quickly monopolized by the General Italian Oil Company, Agip, which presents, against a yellow background, the stylized drawings in black, red, and green of a motorcyclist (product name: "Mas"), a snake ("Energol"), a hirundine man ("Mas" again), or a six-legged dog ("Supercortemaggiore"). On the back of no. 1, however, under two goldfish, is written the following: "A celebrated and marvelous book: Alfred Edmund Brehm's *Life of Animals*. A sweeping and wondrous novel of the real, in which the protagonists are animals, bizarre creatures of prodigious instinct, a manifold mirror to the fabulous fantasies of creation; this famous work by Alfred E. Brehm—German zoologist of illustrious fame—will mean many happy days of reading for you and your children," [continued].

"Wyndham, Wyndham," wind from a dead city, "Heinlein," murmur of a leper, "Dick," drop of acid rain, "Clarke," gulp of a mammoth batrachian, "Sheckley," hand grenade hurled by a Venusian, "Wyndham, Wyndham . . . Wyndham . . ." I wandered around my grandparents' home associating those names with the most beautiful titles I had at my disposal, turning them into undivided syntagmas that I uttered like esoteric formulas: "Ericfrankrussellsentinelsfromspace," "Robertsheckleyuntouchedbyhumanhands," "Charlesericmainethemanwhoownedtheworld," "Edmondhamiltontheshadowedones," "Jamesgordonballardthewatchtowers." I hadn't read those books, but even without taking them off the shelf I knew every detail of their covers, so that to invoke a title meant unleashing its own special abomination. "The House with Black Windows," I dared to utter, and there before me materialized that blood-curdling rat fighting with a little girl over a strange pink object, truly too frightening, better a more metaphysical nightmare than an obscenity like that, how about "The Spheres of Rapa-Nui," there, but no sooner had I spoken these words than I was gripped by a fever of fear against which I was defenseless: and so, bowing my head like a sacrificial victim, I went with my thoughts in search of the most horrible things, and they were the foul blind worms of the depths, the intelligent slimes, the dancing flayed bodies, eroded faces, figures plummeting, grasping, screaming.

Internal advertisements: Predominantly dedicated to the promotion of books, with surprisingly intellectual works for a popular series, which expose the subsequent vulgarization of middlebrow culture. From 1962 to 1969 it is not a rare thing to come across ads that would be hard to imagine today in even the most highbrow periodicals: A Universal History of Infamy by Borges, Fury, Symbol, Value by De Martino, General Linguistics and French Linguistics by Bally, The Primitive Mind by Cantoni, The Crisis of European Sciences and Transcendental Phenomenology by Husserl, Hogarth and His Place in European

Art by Antal, *Three Forms of Failed Existence* by Binswanger, *Phenomenology of Perception* by Merleau-Ponty, *Mannerism in Literature* by Hocke, even 2,000 *Pages of Gramsci* edited by Gallo and Ferrata. And then Jung, Sartre, Lévi-Strauss, Huxley, Lawrence, Woolf, Butor, Leiris, Perec, Kracauer, Paci, Solmi, Kandinsky, Valéry . . . [continued].

While I had all of the covers stamped upon my memory, such that I could run through them, forward and back, as in a catalogue, there were some to which I had to return repeatedly for further observation. It would be precise to say that these covers *called me*. I knew them better than all the rest, yet their beauty and their scariness continually demanded of me a closer look. In front of those images, I would sometimes spend even more than an hour at a time in complete contemplation, daydreaming under their spell, but oppressed, too, by a harrowing sense of the *imminent*. Other times, my gaze was more analytic, in the conviction that certain details would eventually reveal to me the secret of so much scary beauty.

One of these was the cover of no. 253, M. Limat, *The Immortal Statue*: a purplish, partially flooded cave, its towering vault bristling with stalactites; in the background, a hieratic statue; in the water, seen from the waist up, a throng of anthropomorphic creatures, transparent like jellyfish (revealing their skeletons of filamentous fish bones), arms reaching upward with a spasmodic cry of desperation. Causal coagulum of attraction: this very spasm, this very cry (mute, deaf, choked), which, even in my revulsion, inspired in me a heartfelt pity.

Another was the cover of no. 363, Various Authors, *Sci-Fi Stocking Stuffer*: a sea urchin with fingers instead of spines; fingers of men, women, reptiles, birds of prey, monsters. My eye privileged, by isolating them, the worst and the best ones, namely a horrible scaly talon and a few gorgeous feminine fingers with long painted nails.

Another was the cover of no. 266, C. Renard, *Eyes Full of Stars*: an epic duel between a graceful white unicorn and a repulsive monster with bearish-apish limbs, bat wings, and the head of a dragon. Its point of interest was entirely concentrated in that head: encrusted, fissured, rusticated, a senile mouth missing its teeth, and an eye that, despite being red, told you: I am a blind eye.

Short stories: The first Urania made up entirely of short stories is no. 285, R. Sheckley, *Untouched by Human Hands*; the first collection featuring two authors is no. 321, A. Clarke/J.G. Ballard, *Eight Stories*; soon thereafter follow collections by various authors, only the first of whom is named on the spine (option A: D. Knight and Others, *Outlaws of Nature*; option B, more ambiguous: J. Bixby, *"Guardian" and Other Stories*). In Urania's final graphic layout, the tag "The Anthologies" appears when appropriate [continued].

Another was the cover of no. 277, R. Matheson, *Three Millimeters a Day*: a corner in a basement full of filth and rusty objects, a descending spider, a Lilliputian man brandishing a nail like a lance to defend himself. Staring at that scene meant *becoming* that man, whose story of progressive reduction had been told to me, rather unprecedentedly, by my grandfather; nonetheless, the most magnetically distressing element consisted of a bunch of contorted nails right in the foreground, the kind with flat, knurled heads: there, inexplicably, I felt was nestled the *true* fright.

Another was the cover of no. 334, L. Sprague de Camp/ C. M. Kornbluth, *Forbidden Dimensions*: the interior of a wooden building (barn? Woodshed?) perceived from a high angle: a man, hidden in the doorway, watches what is unfolding: over a magic pentagram painted on the floor, an old woman is raising the body of a black hen and letting its blood drip down, while a whitish, rubbery, smoky, wrinkly creature is materializing. The reason for the cover's allure was twofold: certain craggy wrinkles in the conjured being, which made it difficult to understand whether it had a face or not; and the expression worn by the old woman, which combined stupidity with a chilling *faith* in the ritual's outcome. Not to mention those two phono-symbols, "Sprague de Camp" and "Kornbluth," which sounded like a portent of carnage.

But the most looked at cover of them all was that of no. 265, R. Silverberg, *The Dream of the Technarch*. Beyond the wonder of this arcane word, "Technarch," which fascinated me for its archaic and at the same time technological aura (a word therefore charged with an internal distance stretching between past and future), there was in that cover the very image of my own contemplation: a man's face at a three-quarter angle, his eyes staring fixedly at an undefined point; to his side, a large oval porthole looks out onto the beauty of the starry universe, but the man is absorbed, lost in the purest of enchantments; in that possessed gaze I intuited his memories falling into order, the laws of existence being laid bare, and, boring into his eyes with my own, I tried to taste some of that peace. Other times, it instead inspired in me a dizzying sensation, as if my beloved Technarch had come to a halt right at the vertiginous edge of sheer Nothingness, and was looking into it . . .

Introductions: Up to the mid 1960s, every edition is introduced by an editorial note. The introduction to no. 1 begins with the words, "A classic in the genre of 'science fiction,' to use a rather effective neologism . . ." [continued].

For there was this intense quality in the Urania covers: that horror alternated with enchantment, and often the two combined in an ambiguity that consumed me. Hated monsters, adored monsters, how you stayed close to me! And you, bizarre and perplexed little creatures, sleek Lemuridae, ingratiating ectoplasms, disintegrated beings, vampiric globs of energy, and you, crystals, and you, gelatins, and you, philosophic mantises and pedunculated pods, how plausible you were, how perfect you were! How capable you were of melancholy! I close my eyes and I see again an unfettered brain sailing through space, an arctic brigade genuflecting in front of the immense pearly mass of the *Great Kirn*, a lobster-spider right about to clutch a woman who has fallen asleep on the beach, thorny-radial-gibbous forms germinating from the hallucinating forehead of *The Children of Madness*, an eyeball surrounded by rats, a water monster with the face of Donald Duck, a crowd of dismayed figures packed into a crater, a face covered in flesh-eating cockroaches, a liquid being reflected in a rearview mirror, a woman reclining on the first steps of an infinite stairway.

Title translations: Always laudable for the aura they add. Some examples: *The Kraken Wakes* → "The Reawakening of the Abyss"; *Re-birth* → "The Transfigured"; *The Status Civilization* → "The Horrors of Omega"; *The Odious Ones* → "The Children of Madness"; *Metro pour l'inconnu* → "The Immortal Statue"; *Collision Course* → "The Dream of the Technarch"; *The Shrinking Man* → "Three Millimeters a Day". Other notable title changes: *The Puppet Masters* → "The Terrors of the Sixth Moon"; *The Haunted Stars* → "The Shadowed Ones"; *Way Station* → "The House with Black Windows"; *L'enfance des dieux* → "Eyes Full of Stars"; *Of Men and Monsters* → "The Men in the Walls"; *The Day of the Triffids* → "The Horrendous Invasion"; *A Stir of Echoes* → "I Am Helen Driscoll"; *Needle* → "It Slithered in the Sand" [continued].

At the beginning of the '60s, there was a construction company that inundated the city with this advertising poster: a triangle of bricks (that is, a triangular portion of a wall), and on the bricks a black S, stretched out like a snake. Very young at the time, not recognizing that disquieting symbol as a letter due to its elongated curves, I asked my father one day to enlighten me. Establishing whether it was a serpent, a caterpillar, a crack, or something else altogether was a matter of urgency. And he, without realizing that he was about to leave an irremediable mark on my psyche, said, "It's a larva." Questioned on this point, he explained: the walls of our home were *internally* inhabited; inhabiting them, the larvae, unspecified creatures endowed with a migratory faculty, though prone to growing fond of certain walls; incredibly intelligent, these larvae, and attentive observers of our domestic life; finally, they were not evil creatures:

nonetheless, for some people, such an awareness of being known inside and out by the larvae could prove intolerable. Those were his words, "known inside and out," and I was never the same. When, among my grandfather's Uranias, I found no. 521, W. Tenn, *The Men in the Walls*, I knew that my father had not been lying to me.

Author nationalities: Eventually, only English and American writers; but the first few years include several French and Belgian authors (Jean-Gaston Vandel, Yves Dermèze, Pierre Versins, Adrien Sobra, Richard Bessière, Jimmy Guieu, Louis Charbonneau, Maurice Limat, etc.), one Italian (Franco Enna), and other nationalities (Emilio Walesko, Vargo Statten, Karol Bor) [continued].

Taken sequentially, the Urania titles produced effects of saturation, of refraction, of expansion: identical and homologous words chased one after the other, reconnected at a distance, realigned in mutual enhancement, semantic fields expanding, branching out, zeroing in; and the soul of the reader or recollector would emerge exhausted, as if tormented by a musical fever. Families of horror (*The Horrendous Invasion, The Horrors of Omega, The Mountain of Horrors, Horrific Future*) growing pale in clusters of pestilence and mourning (*Horrific Disease, The Leprous Star, The Factory of Scourges, Massacre in the Cretaceous, Agony of the Earth, Lunar Torture, Slow Death*); abyssal obsessions (*The Reawakening of the Abyss, Sons of the Abyss, The City of the Depths, The Slaves of the Deep, The Nightmare on the Seafloor*) becoming associated with the most varied abominations (*The Atlantic Abomination, The Hour of the Great Worms, The Transfigured, The Days of the Monsters*), damnation upon damnation (*The Cursed Planet, Cursed Galaxy, The Cursed Crystals, The Forbidden City, Prohibited Space, The Forbidden Planet*).

But the titles that slid the fingers of disquiet along my heartstrings the longest were those insisting on nothingness, on silence, on oblivion: *The Forgotten Planet, The Lost City, Chronicle of a Lost World, Planet of Exile, Exile on Andromeda, City of No Return, Prisoner of Silence, The Dead Stars, Rockets to Nowhere, The Wind from Nowhere* . . . Knocked over by the harrowing truth that I intuited in so much emptiness, I fell back on more familiar quills, on more sensible snouts, on more logical carapaces: and so I rebounded off titles that were strangely peremptory and falsely neutral (*I Am Helen Driscoll, This Is a Gizmo*), or pompously cryptic (*The Isotope Man, The Stochastic Man*), before landing at last on the one that haunted me the most, the title that I treacherously repeated to myself more than any other: no. 310, H. P. Lovecraft, *The Whisperer in Darkness*.

Para-Urania: Beginning in November 1952, there is *Urania: The Monthly Magazine of Adventures in the Universe and through Time* (discontinued in 1954). From 1971, previously published books are anthologized in the thousand-world series "Millemondi," which first appears annually, then, from 1973, biannually: once in summer ("Millemondiestate") and once in winter ("Millemondinverno"). From 1977, works are reprinted monthly in the "Science Fiction Classics" series. On rare occasions, special issues appear in the principal Urania series: a few instances of "Christmas Urania," and a few editions with a blue, silver, or gold cover.

It Slithered in the Sand was good too, but *The Whisperer in Darkness* was better. Maybe it was the larva who was whispering, maybe it was me, when I would put my ear up to one of the walls in my bedroom. Yes, because even when I had come undone amid all of my grandfather's Uranias, my larvae were still there waiting for me, in my walls. Then there were my grandfather's larvae, then the horrific world lying between my grandparents' home and my own. And then the horrific life to live.

My grandfather died on February 2, 1973, between Urania no. 609 and no. 610. I've remained further back, among the diamonds.

THEY SHOT ME
AND I'M DEAD

That bullet, for how long has it been in orbit? Not even you know, you who in revolving splendor keep it. But I know everything about you, and can tell you that there was a time, many years ago, when a demon slipped into your mind the bloodless enticement of a decoratively graphic phenomenon, which, flying just above the earth's crust, would cover it in ever new curves, like yarn winding itself into a ball: and yet, vanishing through the air, that ephemerally traced line could only last thanks to its unbroken forward momentum. The rapid course of that streaming strand, how you adored it! For you knew it was powered by inexhaustible energy, knew it was turning and returning, crisscrossing the skies above the very places where you, hapless child, lay still. You needed only to think of that orbiting body to feel it spirit you away, as if, with it in flight, you were viewing vertiginously devoured oceans and continents.

But to die—you continued to die in your shoot-outs. Whether you went by "Jack" or "No-Name," you journeyed heroically through the canyons of your mind, melancholy as the dickens: you put all your nobility into your particular way of riding in the saddle, into the crease of your knowing smile: over and over again, without end, you would arrive in immense solitude, get off your horse, tie it to the fence with an abstractly vague knot, and swagger off intensely, recognizing every movement as pregnant with inexpressible and yet precise significance. The leather strap of your holster, the mother-of-pearl grip of your gun, they were sublime, and you were so aware of this that you needed nothing more, and so they could riddle you with bullets there and then, right there in front of the saloon, before any intricate adventure could develop: they riddled you preemptively, leaving everything with its potential intact, you alone knew it—but who else needed to know it anyway?—the beauty of that death lay in its virginity, you died pure, died without your eyes having known the abominable faces of your enemies, which meant you had to die without complaint, jerking with every bullet, then the slow collapse, your eyes staring into the void. But with so much artful feeling concentrated in that climax, your collapse merited a worthier buildup: hence you started over from the beginning, arrived, dismounted, tied up, swaggered, again arrived, dismounted, tied up, swaggered, no amount of slowness seeming sufficiently suspended to you, no allusion sufficiently understated, everything performed with extreme elegance, because the more iniquitous your fate, the more poignantly you'd be mourned. When you were finally down for good, you took one more second to contemplate yourself in your solitude before they poured out of the saloon in a sweaty throng, on the outside triumphant but in truth dismayed, having lost the contrastive significance that emanated from you, you who were its life-giving sun, now extinguished. And so you contemplated your cadaver, lovingly approving its form. Stretched out in the mud, you held unexpressed within you all of your virtues, your unmatched speed: you continued to be the best because they had treacherously killed you by shooting you in the back, and death, taking nothing away from you, adorned you with its terrible majesty. Looking at your body through the eyes of those hayseeds, then, was like dreaming of yourself, and in that glory you found—only then would you find it—in that glory you, child of anguish, found peace.

"They shot me and I'm dead," you commented with the satisfaction that precise things give, and even when that scene had melted away, for a while you went on repeating the same words. "They shot me and I'm dead"—how many thousands of times did you utter this sentence? You would be walking to school, and a gloomy hatred for all your classmates would take hold of you; envisioning for them a thousand different deaths, you worked yourself up into an exalted state that soon putrefied into poison; for a little while yet, you fought, for a little while yet, you raged, and then, at the peak of those bellicose convulsions, you slipped out from under that unbearable weight. "They shot me," you hissed, and already you felt lighter, already the hated faces began to fade; so you repeated, "they shot me," savoring each word, "shot, shot, shot"—and only then, when everything had shrunk away, would you place the final seal on your freedom: "and I'm dead." Now the front door to the school could open and let the riffraff gush out: your corpse was ready, lying in the sawdust before the three front steps, magnificently incongruous with the present.

Or you watched, unseen, the creature who wreaked havoc on your heart: watched her hop on the moped of one especially unsightly character and shuddered, but if you simply whispered your grief, everything aligned with your reveries once more, and the universe became coherent. They, yes, they had killed you, and you, unfeeling and unreachable dust of the earth, remained ignorant of them: defended by nothingness, you were always elsewhere, and never did you—you, who were the fastest of them all!—never, but never did you know a thing about mopeds.

Yet even if that formula was capable of placating you every time you pronounced it, giving you a gift of surprising sweetness, you still had to suffer the thorn of depending on the shot of others. Because all the while, your purest of ends hung on something impure, on human intent, which left a distant hint of itself in the cosmic peace created by your lifeless collapse. Thus, in the name of a more absolute escape from affliction, time after time you daydreamed of a weapon that would shoot itself, simply out of the hard necessity of its metal; a meatus that would open in your heart without any ballistic penetration; a wandering bullet that had strayed from another, faraway fast draw, or from an unrelated, Pollaiuolesque battle; and, finally, your own shot, which, after passing through the flesh of your enemy, would continue its course along the terrestrial surface till, unslowed, it ultimately returned to you from behind—where, sinking like a seed of death, it would at last exhaust its impetus (how epically bitter, how lyrically sweet it was, then, aiming at a heart or a brain while knowing that the true target was the one you carried on you, right between your shoulder blades). Until, blending together these last two scenarios, one October evening you had them naturally converge with that older celestial graffito of yours.

And so you had both bullet and orbit. An eternal bullet orbiting reliably even when you weren't thinking about it or were sleeping, an orbit that was the perpetual date between that metal and your skull. And truly, we wouldn't know how to put into words the pleasure you felt thinking of that projectile while it pierced unhindered through the wood of trees, the brick and the cement of houses, the iron of beams, the ice of cliffs—first the ice and then, deeper inside, the rock. Now it was precisely this flattering enticement that swallowed you up forever: that no hardness in the bullet's path could ever prove impenetrable, that no matter how vast the black bowels of a given material, they could not slow its infinite velocity: and that everything was both easy and arduous, as with all things superhuman, and that you secretly participated in that superhuman immensity like a chosen one, and that thanks to an awesome inconsistency you were simultaneously the rock, the line cutting through it, the bullet, and your own temple, but more magnetically your temple, and that there was an exquisite juiciness to such stylishly traced fatality, and it was the imperfect passion of one of your measly yet indispensable hops in the air. With this exertion, your own personal contribution to the celestial machine ran its course: when the bullet's orbital path was offered to you like a supreme chance, and when the hop was your hazardous way of wanting it and, through your pathetic yearning, becoming worthy of it. For if you didn't put in at least that little disharmonious physical effort, the ritual beauty of those ballistic rotations would have remained unrevealed and vain, and cause for even more tormented longing.

This, therefore, you pretended and pretend once more: to be in a massive assembly, with thousands of people crowded together, and to be the only one who knows that the bullet is coming at a height of roughly two and a half meters, and to await the precise juncture, and to hop—you alone—rising above that uniform expanse of bodies, and to get the longed-for perforation in the head, and to remain thus suspended, in midair, with just enough time to say to yourself

they shot me and I'm dead

and with that, to come apart, disappearing from your own dream, never to fall back down into the unlovable below.

THE HORROR OF
PLAYGROUNDS

There is an area, right beneath the knees of young boys, that encapsulates the horror of playgrounds: there, where the skin is grayer and thicker, almost cooked from rubbing against the grass; there, where the grime has consubstantiated with the dermis. In those livid strips of hide are united all the disjointed undertakings of premature virility, the enrollment in organized mini-mobsterism, and the disgusting logic of the street. The serious and solitary child observes these scorch marks on his coevals and flies into distress; when he hears these other boys' names spoken ("Luca," "Alberto") in concert with that most horrible of locations, his distress only grows: because he knows nothing of those beings, nothing beyond the fact that they exist, and that, under their knees, they have that grayness.

Playgrounds! Inhospitable, steppe-like lands, yet they boast a term of endearment that, if considered carefully, conveys an idea of dupery, of unknowable insidiousness (other false-hoods: the "chestnuts" of the horse chestnut tree, shiny and big but "not good," and you, for your whole life, will imagine for *each* one of those false fruits a slavering agony; the "sand" around the slide, which in its powdery state you can't even recognize as such; the "track"; the "merry-go-round"; the horrendous, unspeakable "jungle gym").

On benches, grouped together in the thick of conversation, sit the mommies: their propensity for complementing one another disturbs you, as you associate the idea of motherhood with singularity, not knowing how to conceive of a maternal benevolence outside domestic confines. To each his sole and inescapable progenitress; and yet in those parks you are perplexed to discover that they—mothers—can also present themselves in this other form, resembling social insects. Often, they interest you more than their offspring, so that you zigzag in their direction on your bicycle to spy on them from up close. They knit, read a magazine with the swashbuckling-sounding name of *Rakam*, they air—oh, horror—air out their feet by slipping their heels out of their shoes, call after a boy to remove his sweater. Their down-at-the-heel chitchat nauseates you, though you have to admit that without their presence any playground would be a savage wilderness. Stuck one to the other like the rings of an earthworm, the mothers represent a reassuring guarantee of order and legality: so long as you remain within their sight, no gang of aggressors would dare knock you off your bicycle and, jumping with both feet, irreparably deform the spokes of your poor wheels, no thief would dare unscrew the top of your bell while his accomplices hold you still, no crazed child would dare squirt you with water guzzled to this end from the drinking fountain and held to this end with an intolerable gargling in his bulging, explosive cheeks . . . And yet, precisely because of this holy guardianship, you would prefer them to be more austere, those mothers, more solemnly enshrouded in their own sacredness; you'd like them to be great and terrible like the Ancient Mothers, chthonic like Matres Matutae.

Along the walkways of those little urban parks, above those lawns, on that ground . . . there, to prove that they are grown-up, which is to say hardened with a disdain for all saccharine sentimentality, for all naïve rectitude, certain browbeaters are given to spitting: truly an incredible thing, the aerial unfolding of the militant gob, which you see backlit by the sun like a rugged comet followed by a trail of minor droplets, and meanwhile you wonder—yes, you, who could only ever do anything remotely similar into the bathroom sink, and only perpendicularly and directly into the drain, and only in private, and only on reasonable grounds, and even then with a certain amount of shame—you wonder how it is that they can plan and then execute something of this sort, gratuitously and in public, going so far as to make it a point of pride, some of them even announcing it beforehand with a barbarous drumming up of phlegm, or rather of thick saliva that wants to pass for phlegm, and the more yellowish and greenish, it is presumed, the more thunderous the clearing of their throats. But no matter how disgusting the preparation and how offensive the implementation, the worst comes after, in the expectoration's permanence on the ground, where a network of virtual lines will link it to all the other spit, new and old alike: a dismaying firmament of the saliva of others, which no amount of caution will allow you to avoid, and how could you—rotating and rotating, sooner or later the wheel of your bicycle will roll over one, one of those excretions, drawing from it a dark splotch that will fade with every new rotation, it's true, and for this reason you'll keep pedaling like a madman, desperately pedaling, even when you want to stop, knowing that even when the splotch blends back into the gleaming rubber you'll still be left with the memory of that contamination, and for a long time at that, until the next gob, and thus your beautiful wheel will no longer be (it already isn't!) strokable with the palm of your hand for the purpose of wiping away stray pebbles, it will be a wheel that was.

Even when they have dried, even when invisible, all of those gobs linger in your consciousness like obscene suspicions: that's why you're so grateful for storms, as it's only in the twinkling that follows a heavy rain that you see playgrounds as places compatible with a child of your persuasion. But no storm could ever wash away the frothy dribble that one day, before your very eyes, a kid spat into his hand before streaking it along the highest part of the slide in order to procure a faster and more lubricious descent: and streak he did, with his damp posterior, the entirety of the innocent metallic slope. From that moment on the slide ceased to exist for you; passing by it, remembering that there was a time when you didn't disdain to climb up on it, you feel as though you are reflecting on the life of a dead man.

There's a place, by the park playgrounds, pompously referred to as "the kiosk" but which you prefer to think of as "the stand." There, you can find things with the power to move you, such as the heartrending snow cone syrups and the archaic ice crusher, alongside other things whose names alone irritate you deeply, such as those prepackaged, mammothrept munchies and spoiled snack cakes, and others yet that pique your curiosity from a scientific point of view, like the little yellow and pink spumoni slices or certain small spirals of flabby licorice.

Frequenting the stand is painful, so numerous are the juvenile customers who expect to be served without dismounting their bikes or removing their roller skates, and such is the supercilious aura emanating from the crowd of kids— as if all of them, when making their purchase, were odiously thinking something along the lines of: It's half past six, the old lady must already be making me dinner, but who cares, I'm a big kid and I do as I please, so watch this, spoiling my appetite is a piece of cake, a truly useless little piece, sponge cake topped with some kind of chemical cream, simply on a whim, look at how I'm spoiling my appetite, oh, look how good I am at spoiling it! And so you—harboring infinite gratitude for your mommy on account of all the soups she prepares for you (you *are* all of those soups), not to mention a sizable amount of guilt, with her far away in the faraway kitchen while you are here, unproductive, so that you would never ever do her wrong by snacking on something outside mealtimes—you manage to suffer for the invisible mothers of those clambering creatures, thinking of them as unwitting, betrayed, scattered in apartment blocks, busy opening useless packets of powdered purée, such honest packets in contrast to which the "kiosk" appears to you an ethically monstrous Collodian creation.

And there is a practice, too, that aggravates your pain: the custom, among the clientele, of calling the vendor "boss." Hey boss, they say to him with a worldly-wise air, at which he winks obligingly. With no appellative other than "sir" have you ever addressed him, always feeling that you are in the right, but with the uneasiness of someone who, finding himself among foreigners, knows he does not have a command of their language.

Away, then, from that South America, quick, down walkways that you would rather were shady but are sunny, that you would rather were solitary but are busy, garden paths that you would like to be Romantic, neoclassical, baroque, Renaissance, but are twentieth-century, down which you can only flee . . . There, on a bench, you never fail to encounter some old man who'll look at you reproachfully, presuming that you are engaged in some amusing fun, you, who have no idea how one even begins to have fun, through which narrow strait one has to pass, when you really think about it, it's a mockery that you of all people should be the one to irritate that old man, though that doesn't mean you don't understand him, on the contrary, your feelings of solidarity with him are all too strong, anyone having fun should never show it to those who don't know and aren't able, what a lewd thing fun is, what an ungenerous thing, the lot of you are young and hardy and that should be enough for you, crouch down into yourselves when in the presence of a melancholy old-timer, slow down your pace, suck in your cheeks and emaciate a bit those mugs of yours, assume a pose that has a touch of the pensive and the austere about it . . . And so I, who never had any fun to begin with, shriveled myself up entirely in order to be a less offensive sight to that old man, and thus stooped, sad as a Bahamontes who just lost the lead in a race to Gaul, I'd make my way to the drinking fountain.

In its little basin, along with Popsicle sticks and assorted leaves, float agglomerations of bubbles that you force yourself to attribute to the inevitable swirling of the water when struck by the fountain's forceful stream. That stream! You monitor whoever drinks before you, making sure they don't touch the brass of the spout with their lips (but you tell yourself that even if they did touch it, the outflowing water alone would suffice to wash the brass; and yet the sight of such contact has always induced you to pass up taking a drink—dying of thirst would be preferable!—as if you were unaware of the myriad unwitnessed contacts, as if those obsolete decorative spouts did not in fact speak to you of at least half a century of unions betwixt metal and flesh . . .). Far better if the child preceding you occludes the low orifice with a fingertip so as to send the water spurting upward, even though, of course, that finger—where has it been, of what limescale and haze does it retain memory? Better to remain in the dark—either way you, too, will drink according to this technique, but with the application of a quite different know-how, first looking at your fingers, choosing one, holding it a long while under the water to wash it, and then, only then, when it feels as polished as a stone in a riverbed, do you place it under the spout like a stopper and finally drink, no longer to quench your thirst, but to dilute the poison that you are.

Gradually, as I make my way back home, the number of friendly countenances grows. Now, sure enough, The Face is coming toward me, while from the opposite sidewalk I receive a theatrical wave from The Tailor; I walk right by The Ogre and The Mummy, farther ahead I recognize The Fake Mother and The Whisperer in Darkness, I go through the main entrance to my building just as The Thing is exiting, and behind the doorman's desk I spy a Triffid and The Vampyre; a damp spot on the elevator floor assures me that The Worm has come home too; I open the door to our apartment, and in the kitchen The Silhouette is handing The Debt Collector his metaphysical spleen.

A rustling of fake dollars coming from my bedroom tells me that Him, The Larva, and Death are getting ready for our game of Monopoly.

If fate should smile on me, I'll take everything from Park Place to Marvin Gardens, and victory shall be mine.

EIGHT WRITERS

There once were eight writers who were the same writer. All of them wrote of the sea and of terrible adventures upon it, all of them used wondrous words like "bulwark" and "bowsprit," all of them knew the farthest geographies, the winds, the fauna, the flora, the constellations, the calculating of positions, extracting from that knowledge the profoundest of woes; they scorched me with the same thirst and the same frenzy, made me shiver from the same tempest, sent me sinking downward under the same exact billow. The ship's hold of which they spoke had a sole darkness, the captain's secret remained forever unrevealed, words and things passed interchangeably from one book to the other with fantastical continuity, and the map . . . the map was torn into many fragments scattered across each of those books, and it was necessary to have read them all, to remember them all, to confuse them all.

The eight names of this immense writer were as follows: Joseph Conrad, Daniel Defoe, Jack London, Herman Melville, Edgar Allan Poe, Emilio Salgari, Robert Louis Stevenson, Jules Verne. Sometimes he told you to call him by one name, sometimes by another: those names were like the phases of the moon, like the many trims of a mast, like the volatile soundings of an unchanging lead. A sentence like "The dawn's gloomy light allowed him to verify how warranted his fear had been: in the small barrel, not a drop of water was left," whose was it? All of them could have written it, all of them *had* written it. Or: "Heavy with rum, they lay about the deck without heeding him," or: "He went back down to fetch the sextant, but in the wardroom he fell in with the massive Chinese mariner," or: "a flickering, there, near the shore, as if from the lagune . . .", ". . . as for the first mate, I had never seen a man more . . .", "who knows if those savages . . .", ". . . giving way with a crash . . .", ". . . a strange mark resembling a cross . . .", ". . . motionless . . .", ". . . from the South-East . . .", ". . . sprays . . .", ". . . signboard of the . . .", ". . . unconscious . . ." And their characters, too, were the characters of a single great book. In the lapping and overlapping of my enchanted mind, Captain Ahab and Lord Jim, Benito Cereno and Silver, Gordon Pym and Captain Nemo, Larsen and Babo, Billy Budd and Jimmy Wait, Van Weyden, Jim Hawkins, Sandokan, Leggatt, Pencroff, MacWhirr, Queequeg, the Black Corsair, and Amasa Delano all sailed in the same waters, crossing one another's wake; they pursued the same prey, dueled to the death for a few guineas or over a rude word; they respected one another, became bound together in indissoluble friendships; wounded, mutilated, wrapped in bloody bandages, they scrambled aboard the rickety planks of their ships, shouted horrible oaths, and all, at once, daringly defied their enemies, the sea's fury, their rebellious crew, the monstrous fish, and the enigma of their own past. Each of them chased indistinguishably after some fanatical goal, devoured by a single obsession, and I was devoured along with them. For this reason, perhaps, those adventures felt so necessary and fateful, and all the more authentic the more they revolved around the same themes with the malleable repetitiveness of a recurring dream. For me, an opener such as "In the year 18— the brig *Rangoon* . . ." was all I needed in order to know that everything was about to start again, and this certainty, while injecting me with a jittery excitement, infected me, too, with the first drops of a poison that, as I read, would spread throughout my organism, together with trepidation and enchantment. Erasing all distinction between life and literature, I experienced the dread one feels at knowing himself destined for scurvy and the rationing of water, for keelhauling, for betrayal, humiliation, death. I might yet avoid shipwreck, or dead-calm seas, or being cut adrift, or mutiny, or pestilence, or desertion: *some* of these things I could perhaps avoid, but not all; at least one of them was in store for me, and to find out which, I needed only to wait. My passion threw itself avidly onto that anguish, adorning it entirely with morbid amazement.

I read as though immersed in a great darkness cut through with bright flashes and streaked with thin trails of light; as when too many colors are mixed together, this darkness was the result of the superimposition of all the excruciating hours spent waiting for a sail on the horizon, all the stranded solitude, all the howling gales, all the dizzy languor, all the descents into the irremeable depths, all the disappointment before an empty treasure chest, all the ruthlessness of chain and blade: an overflowing redundancy, in which those dazzling flares were set off by each sizzling mention of a ship's name, by the idea of a slashed sail, by the image of a Jolly Roger, by the word "hatchway"—little fires that, as soon as

55

they began to spread, were swallowed up in the black, like the heads of castaways submerged under a final wave. And there was a whistling roar within that pitchlike blackening, in which I recognized *his* voices, the eight voices of that protean narrator who knew the ways of my heart through and through. This expedition, one of these voices said to me, is a tale I've already told you once before; these words, another voice said, are ones you've already encountered there, and there, and there too; and another: the tatters covering this figure, are they not cut from the same cloth worn by such and such a character on that page there? And always they warned me that this was this but also that, if not *especially* that, and there was no voyage that had not already begun in a previously read book and that would not continue in a book that was yet to be read.

Those voices left me in a daze, because in my gratitude I listened to each one of them as intently as I did to the rest. I loved them with an identical love, of course, those magnificent murmurers, just as a sports fan loves indiscriminately all the players on his team, from the greatest to the most obscure; and, treating them precisely as a team, I gradually listed their names to myself, and then, as a single man, off and away they went, to cleave the waves!

But the moment came when I began to find there was something desultory in my manner of listening, as if that choral quality—all of those corresponding stories, all of that refraction—weakened the words, and the adventures were losing the plot. The plot twist, the twist of the knife: drama, in a word. So that, little by little, the suspicion grew in me that out of those eight voices, there was one that was *slightly* less authentic, a voice that, by sounding *slightly* off in relation to the others, was blurring the thematic boundaries of things; certainly not from an intention to deceive—I didn't even want to think this—or from a lack of ability, only from a substantive difference of interest: one of them held *other* things close to his heart, one of them had *always* talked about other things, and, having fallen for superficial similarities, I had believed he had called me onto the same pontoons; I had poured that different form of storytelling into myself as though into a mold, without questioning its nature: the error was my own, and the only way to remedy it was to restore that captive to freedom. And while I was still turning these things over in my mind, a name crossed my thoughts like a shooting star. Dismayed by what seemed to me an odious act of abandonment, I wanted to turn back, and for this reason I caressed at length my octet: but now that name had flashed, and I could no longer feign to ignore it. In fact, in the following days it continued to flash like the navigation light of a vessel floating adrift in the darkness: an incredibly long cable still tied him to the other seven, but there was a dignified sorrow, in that far-off flickering, which asked me to have mercy and cut him free. To know that name meant to repudiate him, and it was a good thing, for him as for me, that our paths should separate. So at last I uttered it, and the rope was slashed.

"Jules Verne," I said, and like an inhabitant of Hades, Jules Verne moved off on asphodel-covered waters, a shadow vanishing into the shadows. In the coming weeks, tortured by that parting, I repeated to myself that it had been necessary, because that writer, whom I had loved so much and whom

I continued to love with undiminished love, was not a mask of that many-named other, but an entity unto himself, with characteristics that were too divergent for me to be able to go on ignoring them. Insisting would have produced a gash in the general fabric of the stories, and I feared nothing as much as incongruity. *The Mysterious Island*, that book which I had long associated with *Treasure Island* and with all the other adventurous islands, did it not begin with a journey in a hot-air balloon? An aerial journey, in a "balloon!" Could one imagine anything further from the ancient spirit of those barbarous tales of naval boarding and mutiny, of buried doubloons? Anything more "Parisian?" It was an obvious truth, and yet for a long time I had managed to deny it. All that technological wonder, that lust for modernity, did it not project Verne's books forward, into our own horrible day and age? Not the age of Ahab, not the age of Silver: our time. *Twenty Thousand Leagues Under the Sea* was a beautiful novel, and pages such as those on the coral forest would never be erased from my memory: but in the *Nautilus*'s engines, now that I thought about it, I caught an inkling of a little too much science, like a vague hint of school. I returned to *The Mysterious Island*, and found chapters that opened with summaries such as this one, from the seventeenth of Part One: "Visit to the lake. The indicating current. Cyrus Harding's projects. The fat of the dugong. Employing schistose pyrites. Sulfate of iron. How glycerine is made. Soap. Saltpeter. Sulfuric acid. Azotic acid. The new waterfall." Exhibiting this kind of pedagogical-didactical manifesto as irrefutable proof, I called upon the other seven and silently interrogated them, and Defoe said: No, it is lacking in levity.

And Poe said: No, how glycerine is made—child's play!

And Melville said: No, it reads as though it were written by a German academic.

And Stevenson said: No, adventure is error.

And Salgari said: No, adventure is the Orient.

And Conrad said: No, precision is the death of art.

And London said: No, true knowledge lies in action.

And all of them together added, and it was the final blow, that they didn't see a certain sea—*their* sea, where was it?

I cursed myself for a coward, for I had left it up to them to condemn him. I tried desperately to compensate him, but it was late. Goodbye, wonderful writer, I said. You are a different writer, but you remain wonderful all the same, full of the wonders of saltpeter and pyrite.

So it was that my writer now had seven names, and his stories were without blemish. Wholly congruous, wholly in tune, pulled as tightly together as the fibers in a hempen rope. And seven was so prestigious a number that it placed the works of the elect in a sacred light: the seven pens, the seven keels, the seven seals, the seven syllables of the Name ... However, precisely this evocation of a mystical element was destined to corrupt in short order any possible notion of solidarity. For while I grew used to thinking of those names in revelatory terms, I was led inescapably to consider them no longer as synonyms of equal truth, but as casings enveloping one another in a concentric sequence, from the most external to the most internal, from the least true to the truest.

No sooner had I realized what this meant than I was struck with horror, as if a great chasm had thrown itself open before me. I was still standing there motionless on that vertiginous brink, when a little man appeared, dressed in black with a big white wig on his head.

"To be of service to you, sir," he said urbanely, "that is, to free you of all embarrassment, here is my pen, which I shall place symbolically in your hands. Take it, and I, your humble servant, will return to my native land aboard the first available vessel. As you will no doubt see, this is too advantageous an offer for you to possibly refuse."

"Why *you*, exactly?"

"Because I was born in 1660—truly, a little too long ago for the kinds of things you enjoy. Oh, I know full well that you are a lover of all that is old, and that it is enough for something not to be modern (I will not say 'contemporary,' which is for you a dreadful word) for it to entice you; in this you are possessed by . . . how to put it, by a fanaticism, yes, by a fanaticism of a most singular nature. But you will admit, my gracious reader, that there is past and past—I mean that each kind of past binds us to it in a different manner—and here our discourse concerns the sea, you understand, the sea as a metaphysical dimension of adventure. I use the word 'adventure' in its highest sense and, simultaneously, in its lowest, which are, after all, one and the same. In short, it requires a great feeling for nature and its energy and its enigmas, and an equally great sense of the conscious and the unconscious: it's difficult for me to talk of these things; in my time they did not yet exist. Whyever do you think I am casting myself aside?"

"But your book," I interjected, "is a book of genius."

"A great book, yes, I won't deny it. But be honest, if you remove a few of the opening chapters, where is the sea? The forecastle, the quarterdeck, the yards to brace? And besides, everyone knows that what I really wrote was an essay on economics in the guise of a novel; a seafaring hero must be mad, accursed, sick, whereas mine, ah, *Homo economicus* they call him—don't tell me you find such matters enthralling, the accumulation of capital, the division of labor, all that book-keeping, and admit it, come now, admit that in comparison to yellowed maps and ivory peg legs, the aforementioned subjects have always seemed to you the stuff of philistines . . . "

"But you also wrote a follow-up to that book, in which there are in fact maps, and lots of pirates, lots of raids and mutinies . . . "

"Please don't do me the injustice of such an indulgence. I have sufficient discernment to know that that artificial continuation has no right to represent me. I consist entirely in that industriousness, as I presume you will recall: farmer, potter, tailor, even umbrella-maker . . . "

"But a castaway, too, and once a castaway, always a castaway . . . "

"I appreciate your efforts, but if you should hesitate to dismiss this old umbrella-maker, then the others will surely see to it themselves."

And Poe said: No, it's the stuff of right-minded conformists.

And Melville said: No, it's missing the breath of the epic.

And Stevenson said: No, the road to adventure is paved with dissipation.

And Salgari said: No, fable is luxury.

And Conrad said: No, what embarrassing naïveté.

And London said: No, that guy never left the City.

"See? Now, let's put an end to this and say our goodbyes, for I have a mind to return to my gazettes."

So I said: "Honor to Mr. Daniel Foe, aka Defoe, author of the book titled *The Life and Strange Surprizing Adventures of Robinson Crusoe of York*," and a second before he disappeared, I added, "of Robinson Crusoe of York, *Mariner*."

That, then, was the path I had to go down, sorrowful and piti-less. Just as an inflexible skipper, after harshly punishing a member of his crew, can't sentence to a different punishment whomsoever during the continuation of the voyage proves guilty of the same offense, so I could not stop in my pursuit. Because the truth—the essence!—of seafaring literature was hidden in the heart of that rose, and if the ultimate wholeness was all the way down at the bottom, in its center, I needed to uncover it by traversing the books and the names as one traverses the stormy seas, when out of loyalty to the laid-out course one ignores the outlines of distant lands, and the days and nights become lost in the ship's wake.

I had six names, and one was synonymous with my ear-liest boyhood. That name offered itself up to me unarmed, defenseless in the prominence with which it stood out to me on the large illustrated covers where I had first encountered it. I tried to resist, tried not to imagine him immediately as the outermost layer, telling myself that just because I had encountered him first in my life it didn't mean that now, too, he should be the first; that I could not play into so many clichés, so many loathsome little smiles; that this time it would not be enough to say, "You are a different writer, but you remain a great writer all the same," because any distinction, even the slightest, would be tantamount to disavowal.

Instead, plunging into the deep shame of ingratitude, I lost him. I lost him along with all of my childhood, and the sadness was such that, as a sign of respect, I forbade my brain from enumerating the elements of impurity in his work that would have justified my choice—because his infinite generosity did not deserve that I or anyone else should judge his books, his hundred books all written with the same reed pen held together with cotton thread. And, in fact, Poe kept silent with downcast eyes, and Melville broke his quill, and Stevenson came with a sprig of blooming heather, and Conrad brought the highest decoration of the British Navy, and London doffed his cap and threw it into the sea. And behind them appeared another group of figures, and, with a shudder of both joy and pain, I recognized Sandokan, the Tiger of Malaysia; and Yanez de Gomera of Portugal; and Kammamuri and Tremal-Naik; and the Count of Ventimiglia, called the Black Corsair; and Wan Guld of Flanders; and a delegation of buccaneers from Tortuga Island; and in one voice, they all said: We go with him—and I thought of him in that wood on the outskirts of Turin, all alone with a razor in his hand, and the whole universe never seemed to me so awful. And seeing as a silence had fallen, I felt that I, too, needed to say something, and I said, "By virtue of the powers vested in us by a reader's loving mind, we confer on Mr. Emilio Salgari—although he withdrew prematurely from the Offshore Navigation course at the Paolo Sarpi Nautical Institute in Venice, and has to his credit only a journey from Venice to Brindisi at the age of eighteen, in the capacity of cabin boy—confer on him the captain's license his heart was so deeply set on," and on a little piece of wrinkled paper I wrote "Capt." And the five writers appended their signatures below, and at the last second Verne and Defoe arrived out of breath, saying: Wait, we want to sign too—and they signed.

Thus what had to be done was done.

And so I was left with a quintet, whose homogeneity deluded me for a time into thinking I could indefinitely postpone the next step in that brutal chipping-away. I told myself repeatedly that, for me, life's dark side was depicted by all of them; that all their storms were the selfsame storm, and all their becalmed seas uniformly calm; that in all of them there was the same burning thirst, the same morbidity, the same gloomy and austere exoticism, the same monstrous power to coincide exactly with that crack of sails, that stench of pitch, that mysterious word uttered by a wretched steward, that youth which was always on the point of being lost. Until, one day, I saw a bizarre sight: upon the deserted deck of a dismasted brig drifting in the Indian Ocean, there was a sleigh. Another day, on the shore of a small island sixty miles south-eastward of Celebes, I came across a strange silvery-coated wolf-dog, with eyes gleaming like coals and a long scar on its muzzle; and on yet another day, through the skylight beneath the binnacle, I overheard this bit of conversation between the first mate and the helmsman:

"Yet I tell you it is so, sir."

"I'd say you've been drinking."

"May I sink into the deep if I've touched a drop in the last twenty-four hours."

"Do you realize what you're asking me to believe? Snow! At this latitude and in this season ..."

Then, for a whole week, I was visited by the image of a small fire burning in the immensity of the icy night. At the end of that week, I said, "Okay, come on out."

He appeared with his coat shimmering with snow crystals, magnificent as I had always pictured him, one dog at his left and another dog at his right, tremendous and tame, and likewise magnificent. One of the things I'd wanted more than anything in my life was to play with those dogs, to hug them, to lie on the floor and squeeze them to me; yet in that moment, overcome with emotion, I managed to say only, "Can I pet them?"

"Certainly. After all, it's because of them that you have loved me so."

"Because of them, yes, and because of all the rest."

"By 'the rest' you mean dogs less famous than these, the Far North, trails and campfires, woods upon woods, snow as far as the eye can see ... "

"But you also wrote *The Sea Wolf* and *The Mutiny of the Elsinore*, and all those tales set in the South Sea ... "

"In that case, close your eyes and listen."

And in the silence, he whispered two distinct words, which were "Yukon" and "Melanesia," and it was so undeniable that all his turmoil and all his yearning wished to remain in that first whispered word that there was nothing left to say.

"No one, least of all you, can imagine me without these two dogs by my side, and they're dying to get back to running around up north."

And so I petted them, and was proud to be able to do so.

And Poe said: Art cannot stop at nature; its nature is the supernatural.

And Melville said: The sea is the sea.

And Stevenson said: One had to have lived on those islands.

And Conrad said: Style, dear boy, style.

And the name of the first dog was Buck, and the name of the second dog was White Fang, and the name of the man was Jack.

"And so it seems that Mr. London, too, has left us," observed Edgar Allan Poe.

"And soon you will leave us as well," I replied, before realizing what I was saying.

"And, pray, why *me*?"

"Because . . . because those other three are veritable sea monsters, that's why! I . . . ah, damnation, look at them! Do you think I could possibly . . . Oh, please, why do we have to talk about the reasons for your departure? Would it not be better, for you and for me, to talk instead about what's kept you here until now, the reasons you've remained? Consider this: you were able to witness the departure of Mr. London, who, if we hadn't decided from the start to restrict ourselves to matters of the sea, would have been the last—did you hear me? the *last*—to go, such is the blind love I feel for him. But since his greatness lay elsewhere, we had to tear ourselves asunder. Whereas what speaks on your behalf, in addition to the tale of that manuscript in a bottle, is *The Narrative of Arthur Gordon Pym of Nantucket*, which is one of the most beautiful sea-voyage books ever written . . . crepuscular, delirious, fathomless—"

"I thank you for these adjectives. Adjectives are everything in literature—"

"Agonizing, far-flung, downward-spiraling—"

"Thank you, thank you."

"Claustrophobic, labyrinthic, cannibalistic—"

"Cannibalistic, yes, I rigged the drawing of lots among my castaways to determine who would be eaten first, and you're now doing the same by dealing me the shortest straw. And to think that each one of those three men took something from my novel . . . "

"They all acknowledge their debt to you; for this, and not only for reasons of age, you are a father to them . . . "

And Melville said: I'm grateful to you, but when there's a golden coin nailed to the mast for whoever sees that whale first, there's no time to turn and look back.

And Stevenson said: I'm grateful to you, but I have the suspicion that your supernatural is at odds with the wondrous.

And Conrad said: I'm grateful to you, even if your idea of descent was in need of many corrections.

The Bostonian kept disdainfully silent, creasing his high forehead; then, while he was already walking away, he murmured to me: "I know little words that could annihilate them. What do you say, for example"—here he lowered his voice until it was little more than a whisper—"to 'Pendulum' or to 'Usher' or to 'Amontillado'? But seeing as the supernatural no longer enjoys general favor, I shall keep them all to myself. Adieu"—and with a theatrical cloud of smoke, he vanished into thin air.

*

So at last I had arrived at the point where I had always known I would arrive, at the outer edge of that central core. Nevertheless, in my conquest reigned a sense of loss. Behind me I left desolation and grief, when I turned I saw the floating wreckage of ships and corpses tossed by the waves. The truth! Having agreed to pay the ghastly price of betrayal, I was admitted to its very threshold: I had wanted to see it, and now I saw it shimmering odiously like ice-cold water in a stone tub in the middle of a clearing. That water was inviting me to stay there, to put an end to my inquest. I fell into a contemplative state, like a theologian who, confronted with the Revelation, lets his science drop to the floor like a useless garment. Writer one in three, you who live equally in the heart and on the surface of that core, your greatness cannot be preached, your substance does not suffer numeric characterization. Your perfection is my peace . . .

But from far away, the wind carried to my ears the lament of seabirds, and the booby was saying: If you stop now, they'll have departed for nothing.

And the cormorant was saying: If you stop here, you'll have managed only to cleave your ship in two.

And the pelican was saying: If you stop, how will you justify so much sorrow?

And the seagull was saying: If you won't continue to make sacrifices, you should have never made any to begin with.

And the albatross was saying: Be pitiless, as you have been heretofore. It is the law of the sea.

I turned toward the three writers: their images did not rend themselves one from the other; *his* metamorphic face was continually assuming the features now of one, now of another, now of the third. A formidable covenant united them because they were the greatest, because they were something else entirely, because an abyss separated them from the first five. But even if that superiority equalized them in a sole splendor, I could not stop there. I was looking for a way to leave a scratch on such perfect smoothness, when I had the awful idea of yielding the floor to them, believing that self-love would end up shattering their triumvirate. But with one voice they said: I am I and I am the other two; you have always believed it, so why do you no longer wish to?

Right—why? Why had I reduced myself so, to a furious squall that tears beautiful sails?

"Because . . . because maybe, from a more thorough examination of your works . . ."

And Melville said: I wrote *The Shadow-Line.*

And Stevenson said: I wrote *Moby-Dick.*

And Conrad said: I wrote *Treasure Island.*

And Melville said: I wrote *The Moby-Line.*

And Stevenson said: I wrote *Shadow Island.*

And Conrad said: I wrote *The Treasure.*

And, in a booming bellow of boiling waters, Moby Dick said: Born in Edinburgh, Poland, Jim Ishmael Leggatt, called Billy Budd, took command of the *Pequod* in the same year that the darkness of the *Sephora,* down in the Sea of Japan, convinced Dr. Trelawney—or was it the SS *Nan-Shan,* up off the Chilean coast?—convinced him to trick the captain Amasa Delano with Black Dog's Black Spot so that Falck's tugboat, according to the tale of Herman son of Silver heard in Nantucket by Marlow (a harpoon, I believe) because the secret sharer would yes perhaps a harpoon the ivory of Kurtz

Korzeniowski Vailima Ben Gunn the *Hispaniola* my color is milky white and you insignificant louse would dare to cast doubt on the truth of my novelistic words which are theirs which are his?

When some time had passed, I decided to turn to the most conscientious of the three, and said the following to him: "Immense Conrad, you who know like no other how to stop, right on the page, time's ambiguous pulse and the thousand hues of the sky and sea in that iridescent and rather mephitic mistiness, disseminating the torments of haunted souls; silver-tongued Conrad, you who know better than anyone how to meld psychological analysis and adventure, with the disquieting result of rendering the exotic familiar; subtlest Conrad, who like no other distill morbid decline in the purity of a regal style; yes, you, biographer of shame and anatomist of perplexity: your books taught me that a man's worth must be proved, and that heroic illusions of youth do not always survive when put to the test—the fatal test, that moment which can come sooner or come later, which can be unexpected or foreseen, grandiose or grim, but which surely arrives for all, and when it does arrive must be recognized, because it won't be coming again. You know that trial well, that all-deciding instant: a jump, and the life of Lord Jim was marked forever. Think of Captain Beard, who had to reach the age of sixty before having a command of his own, and of your youth on that ill-starred coal ship; think of Ransome's sick heart and the dead calm in the Gulf of Siam, without any quinine; think of MacWhirr's poise in the typhoon, of Heyst's courteous courage, of the desperate elegance of dying Tuan Jim. And you who created them, you wish to shirk that test? Perhaps I am mistaken, but I believe I have gathered from your stories that, while the shipwreck of one's illusions is dramatic, living an entire life under an illusion is pathetic: and you are not a pathetic writer, you are a wonderful dramatic writer."

And Józef Teodor Konrad Korzeniowski, whom the world knew by the name of Joseph Conrad, said: "I am ready."

And, with my heart at the end of its tether, I continued: "Even though you three are the same writer, I ask you, for my own personal reasons, which are the cruelest of reasons but are by now irrevocable, to separate yourselves, by which I mean to dismember yourselves, disjoining limb from limb and sentence from sentence. And, since it was necessary to start somewhere and I, not to insinuate anything at all but solely on account of your proverbial conscientiousness, started with you, I invite you to choose a name and to contend with him so that from three you might become two, and that two might then be whittled down to one."

And Conrad said: "Since, as a Pole who became an Englishman, I had the writers of that isle for companions and, by the same token, for rivals, I would not be displeased to face Mr. Stevenson, to whom I would appreciate it if you could send news of me."

"Mr. Stevenson," I remarked, "now goes by the name Tusitala, which means 'He Who Tells Stories,' and his homeland is in the Samoan Islands, a place called Vailima—that is, the Five Rivers."

"Then do inform Mr. Tusitala that Joseph Conrad would be honored to be received in the House of the Five Rivers, so that we might test ourselves, one against the other."

I therefore sought out Tusitala, and said to him: "Beloved storyteller, who like a subtle sunlit rain veil the world in an enchanted melancholy, you who must have been touched by a god in the crib, for you employ the pen like a flute and fill with yearning the hearts of men; you, who turn adventure into both nightmare and fairy tale, and who in your pale lunarian delicacy conceal the violence of a flaming star, as evinced not only by that world-famous story of doubles and of monstrous transformation, but also by the hate that tied Durrisdeer and Ballantrae in life and in death; you who were capable of writing *Treasure Island*, a book that, among its thousand merits, bears that of slowing down the growth of whomever had the fortune of reading it in adolescence, which is your eternal age: a book imbued with mystery and yet plastic and solid, a book unreal and yet woody and brackish, a book full of spectacle which I do not hesitate to deem the most beautiful adventure novel ever written, and if I ever have doubts in this respect, I need only think of characters like Silver or Black Dog to dispel them; in short, you, whom I here wish to call by that most musical name of Robert Louis Stevenson in order to connect back to every time I was asked who my favorite authors were and I, even while giving various answers in accordance with age and knowledge, never failed to include you among the elect, always pronouncing 'Stevenson' with grateful exultation—you, I was saying, are invited by Mr. Joseph Conrad to a chivalrous competition, for which the ultimate responsibility, however, falls entirely on my head."

And He Who Tells Stories, smiling, replied: "It seems to me a rather embarrassing proposition, as you will surely agree. But since blushing is the trade of adolescents such as ourselves, well, here I am, I am ready and, I won't conceal it from you, somewhat trepidatious too."

Thus began the memorable challenge between the two cherished writers, who—after one had set out from Malaysia on a dilapidated steamer and the other from the Samoan Islands on a pirogue rowed by four native Samoans—met each other halfway, at a point in the Pacific Ocean not far from the Solomon Islands. There, atop a flat reef just barely protruding from the water, stood a great scale completely encrusted with shells, and the guardians of this scale were the seabirds. Joseph Conrad, who was smoking a pipe full of East India Company tobacco, chose the right-hand pan of the scale and placed on it a selection of his works, which were: *The Nigger of the "Narcissus," Youth, Heart of Darkness, Lord Jim, Typhoon, The Secret Sharer, Victory*, and *The Shadow-Line*; he was also about to set down *Almayer's Folly, An Outcast of the Islands, The Rescue*, and a certain number of stories, but then, thinking better of it, he put them back in his trunk. Tusitala, who was chewing on a magic root, said: "Since you have had the good grace to abstain from drawing on your entire body of work, I will return the courtesy," and with a wave of his long hand he signaled at his four rowers to leave all of his Polynesian tales and the novel titled *The Wrecker* in the bottom of the pirogue. Then he plucked from their hands a reprint of *Treasure Island* covered in childish scribbles, and he laid it alone in the left-hand pan.

Creaking, the scale gave a groan, enduring an agonizing tension; at length the pans trembled in perfect equilibrium, while all around the seabirds whirled, screaming as if driven mad. Then the pan on the left slowly began to drop, and the torture came to an end.

"Of my characters," rung Conrad's gentlemanly voice, "I have always asked that they know how to face the consequences . . . no matter of what. And consequences are consequences. I think I'll go visit old Kurtz down in Africa, at least for a little while. And you, dear Tusitala, I sincerely wish you the best of luck, because you will need it. Goodbye, it has been an honor."

And Stevenson said: I was no worthier than you, but since fate has so desired, I wholeheartedly accept your well-wishes.

And on the horizon could be seen a spout of water shooting up from a whale, and it was a salute and tribute sent by Melville.

It thus came to pass that Robert Louis Stevenson and Herman Melville divided the world between them like the day and the night, and where one man's reign ended the other's began, and the courses of their ships could meet no more: because one was youth and the other was maturity, and one was grace and the other was might—but one was the novel and the other was the novel. And this scission was so profound that the oceans soon couldn't withstand it, and from all the ports of the globe delegations of mariners pushed off to ask the two supreme writers to put an end in one way or another to a situation that impeded all good seafaring men from doing their work in peace; for the fishing boats no longer cast their nets, and the merchant ships no longer carried goods, and the wooden privateers no longer raided and plundered, and the warships no longer fired their cannons, and the whalers no longer hunted whales, and the schooners, the clippers, the frigates, the brigs, the feluccas, the sampans, and all the other types of craft languished, moored in the harbors or at anchor in the bays. Until, one day, Robert Louis Stevenson, who being the more sensitive of the two had noticed to a greater degree the burden of that universal distress and abeyance, reluctantly made up his mind to send his messengers to Herman Melville, and, desiring to act kindly, chose for this mission the well-mannered boy Jim Hawkins and the honest old man Ben Gunn. A month later, there arrived in Vailima two tall and thin individuals, the younger of whom displayed a ghostly pallor, while the other, who had an ivory leg fashioned from a sperm whale's jaw, looked like a man cut away from the stake when the fire has already wasted all his limbs without consuming them. And the one with the ivory leg said, in a cavernous voice: "My master Mr. Melville sends word that with intolerable sadness he accepts, it being no longer deferrable, thy challenge, and for this purpose nominated the here present Captain Benito Cereno and Captain Ahab as his seconds. My master informs thee too that, as thou hast combatted with a solitary book, so he shall forswear all his stories of life among the cannibals, and the novels *Redburn* and *White-Jacket*, and those other narrations titled after the aforesaid Captain Cereno and the hapless foretopman Billy Budd, and rely solely and entirely on the book named *Moby-Dick; or, The Whale*."

Here he fell silent; then, twisting his mouth into a diabolic sneer, added: "If I may tell thee how Ahab sees it, man, thou art already dead," and making a mocking bow, he disappeared with his silent companion.

And I did not know where they would meet, or when, or in what manner they would duel, and I didn't want to know, because my heart wouldn't have borne witnessing such carnage. And in order to be farther away, I fled from the sea and went beyond the mountains, but the storm followed me always, and I knew that it was the island versus the whale, and out of this thought slowly but surely another thought formed, and it was the unequalness of that fight. Because in one of the two books there was the song,

> Fifteen men on the dead man's chest
> Yo-ho-ho, and a bottle of rum

but in the other there was Saturn's grey chaos; in one of the two books was the reproduction of a wonderful map, but in the other was written: "And every morning, perched on our stays, rows of these birds were seen; and in spite of our hootings, for a long time obstinately clung to the hemp, as though they deemed our ship some drifting, uninhabited craft; a thing appointed to desolation, and therefore fit roosting-place for their homeless selves. And heaved and heaved, still unrestingly heaved the black sea, as if its vast tides were a conscience; and the great mundane soul were in anguish."

Then I closed my eyes to focus on Tusitala's noble face, framed by his long smooth hair, but behind that face I saw the gleaming of harpoons, and whirling eddies of reddish foam, and the sinking limbs of torn men, and in my ears echoed the words of the Book of Job, in which it is said that nothing is more terrifying than the Leviathan. Had not Melville himself written that he had neared the conclusion of his work staggering "under the weightiest words of the dictionary"? Had he not revealed that "one often hears of writers that rise and swell with their subject, though it may seem but an ordinary one. How, then, with me, writing of this Leviathan? Unconsciously my chirography expands into placard capitals"?

At dusk on the third day, in the mountain gorge to which I had banished myself, there came looking for me a man with skin as of amber and the gaze of a ferocious beast, and he said: "I, Secundra Dass, faithful servant of the Sahib Ballantrae even in the land of the dead, come deeply bereaved to inform you that it is all over and that you may now return. And to anyone who should ask you for news of this famous trial, you will say that my father, the Sahib Tusitala, is the greatest storyteller of the human race, for that other is a demon disguised as a man; this was understood by us all, men and fish and birds, that no man could have written such a book, for that book is the Apocalypse and its word is ancient like the rumbling of Prophecy and its breath is the rasping of Fallen Angels, and before its preterhuman nature, everything is as the playing of little girls, and before its immensity, everything is but a madrigal. This you will say on your honor."

And I swore on my honor, and, left on my own, I thought of when Tashtego sank into the head of the sperm whale, in the great Heidelburgh Tun full of purest spermaceti: for I, too, had ended up in truth's core and had found the name of names. Secundra Dass was right: that book in which symbols exert on the reader a near physical violence; that book which seems slowly to circle around its theme when in fact it is its theme that is circling around us in increasingly whirling spirals; that impure book which by upending the rules is simultaneously novel, treatise, epic poem, logbook, tragedy, mystery play, ballade; that book which incessantly probes death while chasing right after it, as the harpooner's lance chases after the immense beast; that book of rending and dripping, of howling and lunacy, of torment and damnation, no, that book could not have been written by a man, and for this I uttered "Herman Melville" as I would have said "Aleph" or "Adonai."

But Melville's thundering voice said: "Don't be sentimental, the sea is a matter for practical men. I have sailed, good; I have written a book that you liked more than the others, good; now, however, let's not make such a big fuss over it, because this whole story has gone on long enough. Let me tell you, young lad, you're hotheaded, the sort to become fired up over nothing; and if I may offer you an opportunity to see things from another perspective, well, know that this morning a position opened up on the *Pequod* for a cabin boy."

"On *that Pequod*?"

"Don't ask pointless questions: on the only ship throughout the ages ever to have borne that name. Approximate duration of the journey: four years, should everything go smoothly; for lodgings, a coil of rigging; the pay, nothing beyond what it shall please the cook to pour in your bowl. Well then, do you accept?"

"I'm delighted . . . Of course I accept!"

"Tomorrow at five. We won't wait for you a minute longer."

"And . . . just one more question, if you please: Who will be the captain?"

"Who would you expect it to be? The madman, naturally."

And so, the following morning, at five o'clock sharp, I arrived at the *Pequod* to take up my new duties. On the deck, Captain Ahab and Mr. Melville were busy having a very animated discussion, which was promptly cut short by my arrival; not so promptly, however, to stop me from hearing the captain pronounce these words: "'Tis a mad idea. I wonder how—how it hath sprung into thy head—"

"Oh, speak of the devil," Mr. Melville greeted me. "The captain and I were just talking about you . . ."

Visibly irritated, Ahab was staring straight in front of him, past the gunwale.

"More precisely, we were conjecturing what kind of journey you would prefer; whether an ultimate journey to the farthest ends of consciousness, setting our course straight for the beyond, or a slower and more haphazard voyage, keeping all your scraps of flesh soundly attached to you—I hope you grasp the not-so-veiled meaning of these words."

And I—as I shook with elation at the suspicion that I had indeed grasped it, that meaning—replied: "A slow and haphazard voyage."

"You cannot imagine the extent to which your choice is a cause of comfort for me, but I expected nothing less from a good lad such as yourself. So, the scraps it shall be. Captain Ahab, you heard the boy's decision?"

"Aye, and let me tell thee again: 'tis a mad idea! Hoot! thou hath proved victorious, a thousand times victorious! What more wouldst thou want for us?"

"Indeed, and because I was victorious, I am permitted to do as I please."

"And thinkest thou not of me? A joker, this is what shall become of Ahab, the laughing stock of the inns!"

"You are mistaken, because you shan't have to divide your command with anyone, you have my word. And besides, if I may attempt to cajole your bitter spirit, know that at the point where you now find yourself, you can no longer lose an ounce of sublimity. But avast—go call them!"

With surprising agility for a man equipped with only one leg, Captain Ahab disappeared into the nearest hatch, accompanying his descent with horrible imprecations, while, a few seconds later, with the sentimental air of an old homeowner returning to see his abode after many years, Robert Louis Stevenson ambled onto the deck of the *Pequod*, and, taking it all in, said: "What a wonder of a ship!"

And right after him, with a case full of books of research for a story set during the transition from the sail to steamships, there arrived on the deck Joseph Conrad, who, drying his forehead with a handkerchief, said: "No steam ahead!"

And after him, preceded by sulfuric fumes, there emerged from the hatch Edgar Allan Poe, who, wiping a spiderweb off his waistcoat, said: "The only hell that is also heaven is the sea—it sounds trite, but it is true."

And after him, propped up underneath both arms by two picturesque Thugs, there appeared on deck Emilio Salgari, who, due to the bandaged wound that stretched around his throat, said nothing, and at the sight of the sea shed silent tears.

And after him, wearing a pair of enormous country boots filthy with fresh mud and manure, boarded Daniel Defoe, who, stamping his soles on the plank floor, said: "I've had enough of land-surveying. I can't wait to have a grand old shipwreck!"

And after him, carrying under his arms the cumbersome rolled-up blueprints of a bathysphere destined to revolutionize all knowledge of the submarine world, there climbed aboard Jules Verne, who, tossing the rolls in an empty barrel, said: "To hell with the bathysphere!" and, after a pause, added, "To hell with knowledge!"

Then, despite the overwhelming emotion flowing through me, I found the strength to observe: "We're missing one."

And Melville said: "Mr. London has informed us that he's doing far too well with his dogs to think about leaving his current location. Nevertheless, since it means a great deal to him to be with us symbolically, he has sent us this, with the firm request that it be treated well by the entire crew." And from the hatch hopped out a mutt puppy of extraordinary beauty, shining-black all over, with a white tip on its tail, which began to run up and down the deck. And Melville asked me: "What do you want to name him?" and I replied: "This honor cannot but fall to He Who Tells Stories," and Stevenson said, petting him: "May your name be Osac-Trofic, which we shall agree to pretend is Samoan for 'Heraldic Dog.'"

Then everyone turned toward Herman Melville and said: "Thank you," and Salgari said it with his eyes, and the little dog said it with his tail, and Melville said: "My pleasure," and Captain Ahab, who at that precise moment popped up out of the hatch, commented: "What a disgusting spectacle!" after which he disgruntledly went back below deck to think of the milky white of his whale.

THE BLACK ARROW

In the afternoon, one late spring, the bells upon the fortress of Moat House began ringing out at an unusual hour.

On an afternoon toward the end of the springtime, the bells of Moat-House Castle tolled at a strange hour.

For an entire day, in the library of my grandparents' house in the country, I had stalled over choosing a book. For a month I had read only comics, a mountain of old comics which I reread every summer from the first to the last, whereas that day I had instead awoken with the precise sensation of wanting to read a book. Running my eyes along those spines, I stumbled on titles that had obsessed me for as long as I could remember (horrible titles like *Little Man, What Now?*, *What Do You Think of America?*, and *How Green Was My Valley*), strange titles, titles that intimidated me and others that fascinated me, titles upon titles that, taken all together, eluded me by forming into an impenetrable glutenous mass around which my soul could only circle indecisively. I dithered there as if my whole future depended on my choice, and when I did choose, it was more out of exhaustion than conviction. Or perhaps it was due most of all to a coincidence, one that drew my attention to three books in particular, and, eventually, narrowed my wavering to that triad. Located in rather distant sections of the library, these books were *The Arrow of Gold* by Conrad, *The Black Arrow* by Stevenson, and *White Arrow and Other Stories* by Cooper. I didn't know anything about those authors, but had fallen completely under the spell of a chromatic effect. My happy memories of White Fang and the Black Corsair first led me to rule out the gold; then the power of things sinister made itself felt, and the darkness won out. (A few pages in, upon discovering that the book's subject was an episode in the war between the White Rose of York and the Red Rose of Lancaster, I'd feel quite satisfied at having pulled off three hues in one.)

My long and drawn-out choice had therefore fallen on *The Black Arrow*, which I read with immediate joy and an indecent degree of immersion. After finishing the book at the end of three days, in the moment of supreme vulnerability that always follows in the wake of believing in such fantasies, when from their splendor we are returned to the necessities of our life and have yet to find a replacement for the abundance of significance we've left behind (and, in fact, it seems we will never find one, so quickly and so deeply did we enter into harmony with those daggers, with those crypts, with those spaceships)—well, right at that moment my grandfather informed me that the following day, at seven in the evening, my father would be arriving to stay with us for a few days.

Now, to perceive the pathos in this story, it is essential to know that with the ogreish person of my father I maintained a tortuous relationship composed of paralyzing terrors and paralytic clumps of immense albeit unexpressed affection, of ferocious antagonism and, consequently, of abominable trading in guilt; and that to think of him meant to feel a desperate need to clear things up, only to dive even deeper into the dark pit of ambiguity; meant indulging for but a few seconds in the dream of a communicative eloquence that would finally make up for years of painful reticence, only to know myself newly condemned to silence. If one considers, then, that my father had never before come to stay with me at that house, as a guest of those who I knew were only alien in-laws to him, one will understand why the news of his arrival, while drowning me in anguished hope, had also horribly revived the relevance of my guilt. Seeing him show up in a good mood only increased this feeling, which rose to a level of devastation when, shortly after, he announced that he had brought me a "little gift," which is what, out of dissociative discretion, he called presents. A gift! In August! This fact—heartrending, unspeakable—undid me: as if that display of affection had rendered the ineffable character of my life all the worse. I stood there, stunned, and while my father emptied his suitcase, I haplessly pursued images of the absurd items I might in turn give to him, so as to reciprocate: the stem of a magnolia, a glass full of gravel, the cardboard skeleton of a new shirt stored in my closet—as if consciously conferring on those poor entities a supreme symbolic value could reconcile everything, and not be, again, and forever, a way for mute misunderstanding to triumph.

From across his bed, he handed me the gift: it was a book. Looking at it in my hands, I was dumbstruck. All at once, I sensed in advance the pain it would beget. It was—though seemingly impossible, it *was*—Stevenson's *The Black Arrow*. The first complete thought I managed to formulate was that my great choice four days prior had actually been an awful choice: the worst choice of all possible choices. More pedantic, but more tragic, too, my second thought reemphasized that the disastrousness of my selection was not the consequence of a paternal choice, seeing as that was a subsequent stroke of misfortune, but was the initial, constitutive error (nor was it a relief to verify, as I sneakily did through indirect means, that my father had bought the book that very same day, at a Northern Railway newsstand, for my disquiet had already dilated the gift's meaning into an eternal atemporality).

So that's how things stood. My father had signified his affection with an explicit gesture that, not coinciding with Christmas or my birthday, had something extraordinary about it, almost bordering on indecency; a gesture I could increasingly appreciate as generous, the more I recognized the special unseemliness that had gone into it. Now, this gesture centered on a book, which, as such, not only had its cost (an unbearable idea and fermenter of additional guilt, that someone would spend money—precious *money*—on me), but also an implicit utopic value due to the hedonistic-pedagogical intent that I, the receiver, should procure enjoyment from it, and with that enjoyment an enrichment of my own endowment of humanity. I imagined my father in front of that newsstand, wondering if I would like that book, and the thought of his loving ignorance (will he like it? Will it be his kind of book?) was pure agony. Of course I'd like it, more than you could ever have hoped, but I had ruined everything by *having just read it*, that book, which I therefore could no longer enjoy, not because I couldn't read it again, but because rereadings, apart from needing to occur after a significant interval, should

85

be spurred by a legitimate desire and not, as would be the case here, by the frantic wish to trick both gift and giver into believing that things had gone differently, and that out of all the books of all the literatures of every country and epoch, the same book had not been picked twice. You decided to put your trust in written words that I had already pronounced in your absence, and your affection therefore cannot reach me, for my own blunder, or my own bad luck, keeps me far from it. And then there was that look in his eyes—that sweet look turned vibrant by his nearly imperceptible though implicit satisfaction—with which my father had accompanied the book's bestowal: a look that alone knew how to tear me apart and, in that crucial moment and afterward, in my hounded memory, became unbearable due to my misdeed and, perhaps even worse, my silence vis-à-vis my misdeed. For in keeping my mouth shut I had immediately condemned myself to keeping it shut forever. Having thanked him with feigned enthusiasm, having simulated an impatience to start reading, how could I ever find the courage to tell him, *later*, the truth? Every moment that I let slip by following the harrowing revelation of his gift stretched out deserts of lies; and when, that same night, each with his little light next to his bed, we lay down to read—my father a volume of the *Universale scientifica Boringhieri*, and I that accursed novel, pretending to follow the printed words with my eyes—in that moment, in that bed, in that position, I felt with clarity that the loss of truth, and thereby of all rightness in our relationship, was irreversible. The more minutes passed during that heinous evening, the more my eyes stared blankly at those typographic abstractions, out of fear of glancing up at my father's Caravaggesque silhouette.

Even so, I was capable of this too: of mentally calculating credible amounts of time before turning each page, perfecting, in unison with my deceit, my pain. And when, right before turning off the lights, my father asked me, "So, do you like it?" I remember not knowing whether to reply "Yes" or whether to reply "A lot," unable to determine in which case I would be less untruthful; and having finally opted for a feeble "Yes," I then tortured myself with the suspicion that, through my momentary hesitation, I had led him to believe that the book had thus far left me at a loss, and that my answer had merely been polite.

Over the following days I kept up the charade, with the added anxiety of having to hide what I was reading from my grandfather, fearing that if he saw me with a different edition of the same novel in hand, he would make inopportune comments in my father's presence. A different edition . . . There was, in those words, a seed of salvation that cruel fate had barred me from noticing until after my father had already gone back to the city. I remember that I was standing under the grape arbor, devoured by an atrocious sense of unfulfillment, as if his departure—this, by the way, happened all the time with every person I loved—were his death, and it were now too late to change anything: what hadn't been done would never be done, the unsaid left forever unsaid. Just a few days had been enough for places I had known forever to become crowded with his image, an image that, now that he was gone, had turned into a new shadow cast over those places, exposing them as maimed—them, too, as unfulfilled. And all the while, that thought refused to leave me alone: of all the books of all the literatures . . . I bounded toward the library to try to contain that infinite vertigo; in the end, I did not have a Universal Library at my disposal, for, many though they were, my grandfather's books constituted a mere morsel of the bibliographic catalogue of the possible. I arrived out of breath, counted the volumes on a shelf and multiplied them by the number of shelves, which came out to possibly a thousand in total, meaning the chances of my having visited that mocking travesty upon myself were a thousand to one; or perhaps not, since I needed to factor in the newsstand as well; as far as I could remember they had fifty or so books on display, so multiplying those two figures made it a one-in-fifty-thousand chance . . . No, doing the math had not been a good idea. Fifty thousand was harder for me to imagine than infinity . . .

Suddenly, and no doubt from a shrewdness sparked by desperation, I remembered that very simple and yet deeply complex concept: a *different* edition. Overcoming my instinctive revulsion, I went to take *The Black Arrow* from where I'd returned it after finishing the tale, and brought it downstairs with me to my bedroom. There, on my nightstand, lay the other *Black Arrow*, the one from my father. I rested both volumes on my bed, one next to the other, and examined them closely. They were the same size and both paperbacks, but the first had a matte cover, while the other's was glossy—and on that glossy cover, and only on that glossy cover, was a color photograph of a carriage pulled by two horses, which had the look of a film still. I remembered that on the inside of the first book I had seen printed

Milan, Madella, 1924

I opened the second book and found in small, unassuming type:

1965—Dell'Albero Editions—Turin

And elsewhere on the page, without understanding what it meant, I read

Edited by Alberto Mittone

What could I know about editing, at nine years old? And yet I sensed that this detail was not to be overlooked. If the two editions were truly different, they would be different in everything. I looked in the first book and found

Translation by Gigliola Olivero

"Translation" was a word that made me stop and think. Stevenson didn't have an Italian surname, therefore his novel must have been written in another language, therefore what I had read . . . Globes of joy flashed in my mind. With wittingly wishful thinking I had gone in search of exterior discrepancies that might in some way grant the illusion that the two books did not coincide completely, and now I had found nothing short of a key that promised to unlock and fling wide between them a . . . a distance. Because really all it took was a single different word in the two translations for the innermost substance of the books to be superimposable no more: then I would be able to reread *The Black Arrow* as though it were a new story, and the cosmic crookedness causing me to suffer would thus be righted.

In the book my father gave me, there was no translator listed, meaning it must have been that same editor Mittone, or someone who had worked for him. Whoever it was, I felt immense gratitude toward that person; but . . . but what if, instead, Mrs. Olivero's translation had been reprinted? This hypothesis made my blood run cold. As a consequence, I immediately left the room without having the courage to check. I came back only after dinner, now with the determination of a madman. Sitting on the bed, leaning back against the rails of the headboard, I rested the books on my legs, the Madella on the left and the Dell'Albero on the right. I didn't dare breathe. I simultaneously opened each book to page 5, where both—discouraging coincidence—began the narrative. Now everything would be decided. On the left I read "In the afternoon," on the right, "On an afternoon." I was safe! *An* afternoon is not *the* afternoon: it's like saying on a day, a particular day, whereas *in the afternoon* means the afternoon and not the morning, the afternoon and not the evening. My father's book was already shaping up to be the vaguer of the two; but then, right after, as though to compensate, the tables were turned: *one late spring* indicated one among many springs in the Middle Ages, whereas *the springtime* intended, rather, to exclude the other three seasons; in the first instance, the focus was one out of a great number of seasons (how long had the Middle Ages lasted? Years and years and years, maybe centuries), in the second, it was one season out of four: over there, the time frame related to chronology, over here, to weather (this discovery pleased me so much that, moving my head in quick jerks from left to right and vice versa, I reiterated like a lunatic,

"Chronology-weather-chronology-weather"). Yes, they were already two different worlds. Furthermore, the spring on the left was *late*, an adjective that caused one's heart to ache, while on the right, more discursively, it was *toward the end of the springtime*: irrespective of tone, this also meant that, as far as Mrs. Olivero saw it, the story potentially began as early as late April or the beginning of May, whereas if I went by the other translator, I would have to move closer to the season's *end*, fast-forwarding to its final days in June. Here, I suddenly doubted whether it was right to go on splitting hairs in the calendar, or if it would be better to search instead for something deeper, something that I might have brushed past without granting it the attention it merited. I retraced in reverse the latest bends in my thinking, and understood that I needed to probe further into that heartache. I deduced that the adjective "late," in evoking something belated or delayed, was an adjective of regret, and that "toward the end," which suggested the reaching of a conclusion, was an expression of fullness: hence, in the one case—with that first inflection descending through every branch of the story—it was a melancholy tale, and in the other, a tale of adventure. And, insatiably insisting on this point: over there, pensive and inward-looking characters (even if, to be honest, that wasn't exactly how I remembered them), over here, sprightly warriors. This contrast now did not spare even the physiognomy of the translators: pale and kind Mrs.—nay, Miss—Olivero, vigorous and hot-blooded Mr. Alberto Mittone, a little brutish even (he translated and drank from an enormous tankard, translated and cursed, translated and pounded the table with his fist).

And yet the kind young lady then went on to use a word like "fortress":

> *In the afternoon, one late spring, the bells upon the fortress of Moat House began ringing out at an unusual hour.*

undoubtedly harsher and more warlike than Mittone's "castle":

> *On an afternoon toward the end of the springtime, the bells of Moat-House Castle tolled at a strange hour.*

Because a castle—it seemed to me—might well be a place of war, but is also a place for jousting tournaments, dances, feasts; while in a fortress there is no life but at arms: which is why this structure will be vertical and turret-studded as much as the other will be expansive and horizontal, with various courtyards and loggias on the inside (as exemplarily demonstrated by the Sforza Castle in Milan); this one perched on a rocky and inaccessible peak, the other planted in a plain or on a hillock; finally, charcoal-colored will be the fortress, reddish-ocher the castle. With confidence augmented from my success thus far, I abandoned this particular prey, even though I knew I could have gone on bleeding it dry, to proceed further:

> *In the afternoon, one late spring, the bells upon the fortress of Moat House began ringing out at an unusual hour.*

> *On an afternoon toward the end of the springtime, the bells of Moat-House Castle tolled at a strange hour.*

So, according to the book from 1924, there began a prolonged, insistent ringing; according to the one from 1965,
there was an isolated toll, maybe a single chime. Signals, one
more frantic, the other more peremptory, which might have
been sounded by a distressed friar and by a mean gendarme
respectively, signifying in one case a call for help from the
besieged monastery and, in the other, the announcement of
a public execution. Or maybe "ringing out" didn't indicate
a repetition of the sound so much as its expansion through
space, its resounding echo, as though the stress fell not on
its original sonorous quality but on the impression it evoked
in listeners, with an overall effect that was undoubtedly more
disquieting—even if I then had to admit that, in its spareness,
"tolled" was perhaps the more dramatic verb. Either way, in
both translations the sentence continued, and ultimately
concluded, under the sign of mystery:

*In the afternoon, one late spring, the bells upon the fortress of Moat
House began ringing out at an unusual hour.*

*On an afternoon toward the end of the springtime, the bells of
Moat-House Castle tolled at a strange hour.*

I wondered whether the *unusual* hour or the *strange* hour
differed more from the normal hour (it, too, mysterious),
arriving at the conclusion that if the first adjective was more
elegant and precise, and therefore more beautiful, the second
opened the door to a more fantastical perspective, with that
strange hour potentially being even a twenty-fifth hour, the
hour of another dimension, a non-hour.

The non-hour! And only in my father's book! But I knew that the aim of that comparison was to establish not the superiority of the new book over the old (now that the first sentence was finished, I could if anything claim the opposite), but their differentness, whatever it consisted in, and the reading of the second book as something altogether new and, indeed, original. Only in this way would my father's gift be received as it deserved to be; only with an impassioned reading, or rather, with a *satisfied* reading, would I meet expectations. And that difference—as a reward for having imagined it, I had attained it. Just to be sure, I put in the effort of extending my comparison to the entirety of the first page, a task to which I dedicated the following morning; then, without a shred of doubt left, I put the Madella edition back in the library and read only the Dell'Albero. I read the story as though for the first time, experiencing all the suspense of expecting an adjective but knowing not which one, the surprise of bumping into a plumed adverb in the night, the comfort of spotting the heraldic quarters of a semicolon, the armor of italics, the livery of a conditional. And making my way through the novel, I felt that I was sending affectionate messages to my father, like that knight who, at the end of every day of his journey, sent an envoy to his king, and as the length of his journey grew by the day, so grew the number of envoys. A few pages before arriving at the end of the book, I thought of calling my father on a random pretext just to tell him that I had come to enjoy the book more and more, that maybe at first I hadn't thanked him enough, that inside there was even a non-hour, that Moat-House was written with a hyphen, that I wanted to know if he had read it too, and if that was why he had chosen it . . . I wanted to say all of this, and much more, to him. But I didn't tell him a thing.

———

On a certain afternoon, in the late springtime, the bell upon Tunstall Moat House was heard ringing at an unaccustomed hour.

JIGSAWED GREENS

The first puzzle depicted an Andean landscape by an anonymous Spanish painter from the nineteenth century, seven hundred and fifty pieces. My mother was the architect and the forewoman, I a stonecutter. My tasks were only menial: gather all of the sky-blue pieces into a corner, look in the box for a certain trefoil piece, reposition the cover displaying the image. With didactic zeal my mother provided commentary on her own work in order to reveal to me the method underlying it: not to rummage chaotically in the box, but scrupulously comb, flip, isolate; subdivide certain categories of pieces by hue or by grain, placing them in mugs, saucepans, saucers; gently lay the piece in its place without trying to force it; first compose the frame, then the easier figures, starting with their contours, and then, finally, the sky and the fields, starting with the horizon line; know when to stop insisting on resolving a given area in order to open a new front; remember that, as a general rule, a quatrefoil piece will tend to fall in a central square with sixteen pieces on each side; alternate a negative view with a positive view, dialectically tempering the search for fullness in known empty spaces with the emptiness of known full spaces; avoid relying on the initial compatibility of shapes, colors, and lines, but skeptically suppose, as a precautionary measure, a diabolical coincidence, and in the absence of absolute certainty, abstain.

A school of rigor, the rigorousness of that school . . . I had the privilege of placing a piece only toward the end of the next puzzle, a thousand-piece Hans Holbein: the fifth-to-last piece was granted to me, with a margin of uncertainty and responsibility that, while leaving intact the ease of this debut, did not in any way attenuate my nervousness. In order to put that piece in its place, I had needed to learn to hold it by the edges as one holds a photograph: lowering it, I had the sensation that it was melting into the painting like a drop of mercury. The correct insertion of that piece marked my initiation into the sublime discipline, the severe charm of which would reveal itself to me by degrees until the point where, as happens in the study of ancient Greek or algebra, proficiency strips itself of technique to become an animalistic source of pleasure. My mother, as is well known, was a virtuoso, a true jigsaw monster: in the span of two years, I acquired a sufficient amount of skill to keep her busy with competitions that, though still ultimately ending in her favor, were never completely free of uncertainty. By the start of the third year, I had reached her level. When three more years had passed, at the very moment when I brilliantly unraveled the arduous exegetic knot of a false shadow cone in a four-thousand-piece Altdorfer, she told me that I had become the best. Moved, I denied it; she hugged me, confiding that from my very first attempts she had been sure that it would happen, she had prophesied my glory upon crossing that last threshold, entering into that elysian rarefaction. Now that I'm alone and that threshold has long been crossed, I know that for a few seconds in her life she must indeed have had a fleeting vision of my destiny, so brightly did her eyes light up when she talked to me of that fantastical husk, the dissolution of technique, the absolute purification of the gesture, the physical, pre-mental knowledge of any given piece's fate, its immediate positioning, not in the economy of full and empty, but in the nakedness of space, at the single correct intersection of virtual coordinates.

I am often visited and overwhelmed by the simultaneous memory of all the puzzles assembled before arriving where I am now: Cézanne, Pontormo, Corot, Zurbarán, Friedrich, Vermeer, Morandi, Klee, Pisanello, Van Gogh, Bruegel, Rembrandt, Goya, Van Dyck, these puzzles were also a way to learn art history in a non-scholastic fashion, through details and the physicality of the brushstrokes; in this, my mother showed the way unwaveringly, giving me to understand from the very beginning that any non-painterly subject would have had such a vulgar effect on our discipline as to deprive it of all sense. Out of a kind of discretion, in which pity and disgust were mixed as well, she never spoke to me explicitly of puzzles with photographic subjects, but I knew that her periphrases were alluding to those abominations, and the idea of such baseness disturbed me. Her intransigence immediately became my own: no less embarrassed, I still cannot lay my eyes on one of those boxes without feeling as scandalized as the Church Fathers before a heretic.

My mother, who for many years had kept herself above the five-thousand-piece range, came back down to inferior levels for the time required for my education. Having climbed back up to five thousand, filled with fresh youth, she could barely contain the fever inside her, and after letting me familiarize myself with that altitude, she pulled me along with her to new heights. Eight thousand, ten thousand, twelve thousand pieces, the highest she'd ever reached. She'd talked to me about that old twelve-thousand-piecer so many times that when she brought it down from the crawl space, and I understood that we would reassemble it together, I felt as though the very roots of my destiny had been replanted. It was Grünewald's great polyptych, known as the Isenheim Altarpiece; begun on the night of Christmas Eve, and conducted at a rate of two thousand pieces per day, it was finished, and immediately taken apart, by the end of New Year's Eve. This was another one of the fundamental laws of the art form, last in the order of application but first from a logical and ontological point of view: the puzzle could not be considered completed and actualized until after its disassembly, and, more precisely, its *immediate* disassembly; and so it followed as a corollary that every instant spent stalling, after the placement of the last piece, was to the detriment of the sense and thereby the value of the entire execution, as though to call into question its absolute gratuitousness. Upon an awareness of such gratuitousness is founded, piece after piece, the pleasure and the pride of the practitioner, who in this pointlessness purifies their spirit, unburdening it of the heavy load we are allotted at birth. Because of this, one should undertake a puzzle not "to pass the time"—which would still be a form of justification and profit *ab externo*—but only out of love for the undertaking in and of itself, just as whosoever opens a book for anything other than the sheer pleasure of reading does not know what literature is. And so

I learned this truth from my mother: that the most suitable moment to start a new puzzle is when we are overwhelmed with commitments, in the frantic urgency of serious things, of solid things: what a triumph over the world, then, to dedicate oneself to that scientific squandering of time! But, again, for its uselessness to be perfect, the work must necessarily come apart at the very moment it is completed and, in becoming complete, reified. Whoever defers its destruction no doubt does so in order to contemplate the result a little longer, but as much as the act of contemplation might delude us into thinking the opposite, it is never disinterested. We know in fact that the sight of the recomposed painting, far from remaining a neutral experience, infects the puzzler with the impure notion of having acted in order to reach *that* goal—again, contemplation itself—and not out of a devotion to the beautifully useless, to that particular ideal of the beautiful-methodical-useless here being discussed. Nevertheless—and of this, too, my mother informed me through tactful circumlocutions—there are people out there who complete a puzzle and leave it on the table for days, at the mercy of their own eyes and the eyes *of anyone else.* And there are even more depraved persons *who never take them apart,* and for this reason *glue* all of the pieces onto cardboard or thin plywood. And, finally, individuals who go so far as to *hang* that horrific thing on a wall, that aberration which is a glued-together puzzle.

Yes, the orthodoxy of the puzzle was threatened by those obscenities—the photographic heresy, the preservative heresy, the adhesive heresy, the hanging heresy—and to better confront them, my mother and I not only respected the law, but practiced an even more restrictive interpretation of it. According to this interpretation, the puzzle is *never* to be exhibited to extraneous eyes, not even by accident, but, as something secret indeed, must remain visually unshared throughout the course of its existence. To this end, considering extraneous even the closest of family members, it is necessary for the possessor of the puzzle to carry out the puzzling activity in a closed room to which all access is denied; and in situations when prohibiting access proves impossible, supremely advisable is the custom of covering one's work, during breaks, with a silken shroud.

Thus the devotee knows himself called to practice a solemn solitude, for only in solitude will the rustling of those minuscule pieces be transmuted into a sermonizing whisper. The puzzles we assembled as a pair, my mother and I working as a single unit, were one thing; but when she or I each had our own personal puzzle, never would the other presume to help, nor even loom over the puzzle with a glance as if to hint at having spotted a move. Still, when passing by the other's unattended work, it was almost impossible to resist the temptation to insert at least one piece: in which case, however, it was a matter of ethical necessity to remove that piece before leaving, placing it back whence it was plucked, and then in good time to notify the other, "I put a piece into yours. I took it out again." Both of us, in any event, had developed such a mastery of the art form that not even the slightest alteration would have escaped us.

Solitude . . . The solitude of the prisoner, the solitude of the demiurge. Following in those maternal footsteps, I learned the fragmentary nature of the world and the discontinuity of being, learned guilelessly the ways of gnosis, learned that no knowledge is granted that does not lead the multiple back to the singular or give form to what is formless; that there is something fairy tale-like about monads, because no fragment can ever exhaust the greater pattern; that every entity decays when unseated from its proper place; and finally, all the while, that not just any quality or essence contributes to the meaning of the cosmos, but only the principle of quantity as expressed in computable sums and illustratable series. Juxtapose, associate, tie by congruence of shape, facilitating analogies and exalting compatibilities! Deciphering enigmas not along the mystical road of philosophers and theologians, but with the spirit of the cartographer and the archivist, of the lexicographer and the naturalist! Understanding that the great sage was not Plato but Ramusio, not Hegel but Linnaeus! Blazing an analytical trail to Faustian endeavors! For this, for this mirage of a horizontal extension of knowing, larger and larger puzzles were needed.

In Italy, it was impossible to find puzzles with more than twelve thousand pieces. After exhausting everything available on the market, my mother and I soon found ourselves in the pitiable condition of having to wait for a manufacturer to distribute new twelve-thousand-piece boxes; since this occurred at a considerably slower rate than our speed of execution, it followed that if we didn't want to go too long without, we had to fall back on ten-thousand- or eight-thousand-piece models which were, by now, verily humiliating. Of course, we could have returned to previously completed twelve-thousand-piecers, but redoing puzzles was too delicate a proposition for us to be able to introduce it so nonchalantly as a topic of discussion; while not sharing the intransigence of the great masters who had publicly declared their opposition to any repetitive scenario, a redo was still something too dubious for the two of us to implement without a sense of uneasiness.

When, in a specialty catalogue, we learned of a fifteen-thousand-piece *Temptations of Saint Anthony* produced by a small Alsatian company for the bicentenary of the Museu de Arte Antiga in Lisbon, we immediately ordered two sets, which we proceeded to assemble, each of us independently, with supreme satisfaction; on that occasion, I beat my mother by a day and a night. Then came a twenty-four-thousand-piece *Night Watch*, purchased over the phone from an auction house in Buenos Aires; the catalogue hadn't included any information on the manufacturer, so it was a true revelation, upon opening the package, to discover that it was one of a kind, realized by an artisan in 1930, for a Uruguayan connoisseur. We had already experienced Rembrandt's painting in a five-thousand-piece incarnation; the difference was so great that we reciprocally swore that we would leave no stone unturned in our pursuit to procure ourselves a similar pleasure once more.

So began our financial ruin. We became intimately acquainted with art photographers, printers, and die cutters, whom we commissioned to produce every one of our old dreams: Sironi's *The Gasometer* in eighteen thousand pieces, a detail of a Fattori representing the rump of a horse in twenty thousand, an India ink and wash drawing by Kubin in twenty-five thousand, a Velázquez and a de La Tour in thirty thousand, Rogier van der Weyden's *The Last Judgement* in forty thousand, Duccio's *Pietà* in fifty-eight thousand, a stormy dawn by Turner in seventy-two thousand. And just as those mountains of pieces were never high enough for us, there was never a table that could provide us with a sufficient foundation for our work. Ten thousand pieces already cause considerable problems in terms of space: going beyond that limit means having to turn to suspended surfaces and movable hoists, or else working directly on the floor, or even, when the floor itself isn't up to the task, to accepting that the puzzle must be subdivided into sections to be executed separately in different rooms or at different times. And so, down narrow walkways squeezed between the mosaics and the scattered tesserae, we wound our way through our home like byzantine tile layers, in atmospheres perpetually permeated by the suspension of cardboard dust that every puzzle leaves as a kind of residue; I have the suspicion, no, the certainty, that this aerial plankton did not do our health any good—but we moved through it with light hearts, and when illuminated by the sunlight, it seemed to us a . . . a call.

Our crazed quest for perfection knew no limit. While for many years we had kept up the habit of forgoing looking at the puzzle's reference image (such that we would blush at the thought that there had been an earlier era in which we'd indulged in that vulgar practice), and, in conjunction with the dearth of twelve-thousand-piece puzzles, had resorted at times to the expedient of mixing together two identical six-thousand-piecers (which, not actually being identical—due to the unrepeatability of each die cut—did not provide for an interchangeability of pieces, multiplying instead, what with the necessity of distinction, the ambiguous intricacies of our

104

undertaking), at this point my mother and I ventured further still in our exploration of increasingly fantastical paths. We ordered four twenty-five-thousand-piece puzzles, each one depicting a different Madonna by Giambellino: pouring them into a single container, we then experienced the intoxication of assigning all of those blues to the four similar but different panels. Then we decided to realize a puzzle checkered like a chessboard, skipping every other piece so that only their corners touched: tested with a twenty-thousand Sebastiano del Piombo, the method was perfected with a thirty-eight-thousand Gauguin, and on that occasion we put together a second chessboard too, a complementary negative of the first. We pushed so far in this direction as to establish the placing of pieces according to a complex algorithmic sequence—but of this experiment, the subject of which happened to be a simple ten-thousand-piece Seurat, I retain no significant memory. And, naturally, we executed puzzles flipped face down, of every size and quantity; to elevate this difficulty to its full potential, we eventually ordered a puzzle cut from bilaterally gray cardboard, polished and glossed on both sides. Faced with the impossibility of increasing the number of pieces to infinity, a kind of subtractive mania took hold of us: having first erased the image, it was inevitable that we would come to the complete erasure of any visual dimension, which we brought about by operating in the dark, through mere tactile perception. Down this road, however—and it's something I can't reveal without a certain amount of pain— my mother was unable to follow me all the way. For my own part, I went so far as to work with a pair of gloves in order to mortify the faculties of my fingertips.

Between one puzzle and the next, we tended to fill our days with mnemonic exercises, the most elementary of which consisted of this: taking a piece from one of the hundreds of boxes, she or I would invite the other to identify its provenance; the answer was to be articulated in the following manner: "Paul Cézanne, *Norman Landscape*, oil on canvas, 1891, Kunstmuseum, Berlin, thirty thousand units, fragment of oak trunk"; "Simone Martini, *Maestà*, fresco, circa 1315, Palazzo Pubblico, Siena, forty thousand units, fragment of the Archangel Gabriel's halo."

I see it has truly gotten late. There are still many more things I could recount, but I haven't the will nor the time. I'm telling you, it's late.

From so many memories, from all of my memories, I choose to bring with me into the nothingness ahead that courteous rustling, the cracks in the gold of the medieval panels, the mysterious, pale sweetness of certain jigsawed greens.

WAR SONGS

The premise of this story is that few things, in the vast and sorrowful world, are as heartrending as the songs of the Italian mountain infantry, the Alpini. Whosoever doesn't feel the same way is free to read no further.

Of all those songs—which in my mother's inspired voice accompanied my entire childhood, often taking the place of lullabies or fairy tales—one in particular had and continues to have for me a supremely saddening power: I'm referring to the sweet and sublime epic-lyric "Monte Canino," about which my spirit nevertheless does not know how to write, as though its superhuman beauty placed it beyond all commentary. From so much emotional devastation, may there now reappear, in homage to bygone days, only the musicless words:

> Do you remember, April was the month,
> That long train ride toward the front
> Carrying with it thousands of Alpini:
> Come, run, the hour has come to leave
>> Carrying with it thousands of Alpini:
>> Come, run, the hour has come to leave.
> After three days of railroad tracks
> And two more of an endless trek,

On Monte Canino we've now arrived
And must rest beneath the open skies
 On Monte Canino we've now arrived
 And must rest beneath the open skies.
No more blankets, pillows, and sheets,
Nor your kisses, intoxicatingly sweet,
There's only the sound of birds of prey
And the rumbling of cannons farther away
 There's only the sound of birds of prey
 And the rumbling of cannons farther away.
If you are hungry, look far off,
If thirsty, in your hand take a cup,
 If thirsty, in your hand take a cup,
For the snow will come to refresh us
 If thirsty, in your hand take a cup,
 For the snow will come to refresh us.

After "Monte Canino," the song that best knew the secret ways of my heart was "*Il testamento del Capitano*," or "The Captain's Testament." On this one, as indirect compensation for my silence on the first song, I will be happy to dwell. Though I won't speak of the violent emotion it used to kindle in me, but only of certain tortuous, unsatiated reveries concerning those five famous pieces.

The first part of the song was gentle, devastating yet gentle:

The Captain of the company
Is wounded and will soon die.
He sends word to his Alpini
To come back to his side.

> His Alpini send word back:
> They haven't shoes to walk.
> With shoes or without shoes,
> I want my Alpini here.
> What commands our Captain
> Now that we are near?

He wanted *his* Alpini and he wanted them *there*; he wanted them at all costs, *with shoes or without shoes*: in that pathetic imperative was condensed all that was sweet and all that was doleful in those first lines—to command one last time, to order a pitiless act only to testify to hidden affection, to be Captain up till the end so as to begin to be Captain no longer. But so much urgency suggested that there was something else, too, at work in him, something strung between hope and desperation, an obsession that was already delirium, surreal raving:

> And I command that my body
> Be into five pieces cut.

Five, not a piece less and not a piece more. That fantastical precision gave me a strange pleasure, the same that, growing up, I would learn to recognize as the pleasure of literature. Five pieces: thus spoke the Captain in his poetic agony, demonstrating just how equitable his rigidity was after all. But the song, like all things magical, was elusive, and in the second verse it reaffirmed itself in the form of mystery, a mystery that only ran deeper the more it dressed itself in the contrary ways of orderly commands:

> The first piece to the fatherland
> To remind it of its soldiers,
> The second piece to the company
> To remind it of its Captain,
> The third piece to my mother
> To remind her of her Alpine son,
> The fourth piece to my beloved
> To remind her of her first love,
> The final piece to the mountains
> To bloom there with flowers and roses
>> The final piece to the mountains
>> To bloom there with flowers and roses.

Now, these pieces, which at first entered one's thoughts as rather abstract entities, upon closer consideration became reified as physical chunks, before, upon even more prolonged meditation, becoming tinged with reddest blood. And so it was flesh, but not so much flesh as butchered meat—scandalously live, scandalously dead meat. I imagined them, five fifths of Captain, all lined up on a military tarp in front of an empty tent, or maybe stuck individually into five backpacks or ammunition boxes, and I was the sentinel who had to keep watch the whole night lest anything happen to them, until the moment came when the lieutenant would assign them to the five men appointed to deliver them. For even if I didn't linger on how they went about the butchering, even if I disregarded the methods of preservation (for which one could intuit salt, snow) and storage, there still remained that void, the enigma of those unexplained datives which, though ostensibly reflecting a wholly symbolic dedication of the self, something, something deeper in the song, impelled me to interpret literally, as the material destinations.

And so came the long and perilous journeys of the five bearers, each in a different direction, through the trenches and along grenade-ravaged summits, behind the front lines and through the field hospitals, with a special safe-conduct that silenced the commanders of any sentry posts, all possible respect and aid had to be given to that man there, on the double, his mission was sacred. But I knew that allowing myself to get lost dreaming of those missions—all those rainy nights, and all that barbed wire and booming in the distance—was only a way of avoiding the actual preoccupations with which the song bedeviled me, and which concerned even more directly those addressees and the pieces themselves.

The first of these two categories disconcerted me on account of the dissimilarities within the group, which I broke down in the following manner:

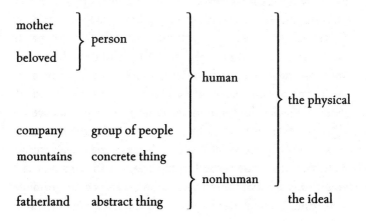

mother ⎫
         ⎬ person
beloved ⎭   ⎫
                      ⎬ human
company group of people ⎭   ⎫
                                    ⎬ the physical
mountains concrete thing ⎫   ⎭
                            ⎬ nonhuman
fatherland abstract thing ⎭   the ideal

Such multifariousness, beyond conferring on the whole plan an aura of scant credibility and feasibility, immediately created other brainteasers whereby one had to stop and reflect on the location of those heterogeneous subjects. The mother and the beloved, whom I liked to imagine in two different but nearby villages in the province of Belluno, posed no particular problem; nor, least of all, did the company, which was established as having already gathered together at the Captain's deathbed. But by "mountains," was he referring to the ones in which the scene was unfolding, or all the mountains across the entire theater of war, or the mountains of his youth, or mountains in general? For which summit, for what pass, would the bearer of the fifth piece set out? And, finally, there was that abstract thing called the fatherland. Was it in Rome, on the steps of a symbolic monument? The idea repulsed me: I preferred it to be that same maternal village, or any given point along the Italian–Austrian border. Had they been ashes, I would have pictured them being scattered by a gust of wind, in front of that empty tent—but the song spoke of pieces, cut-up pieces of flesh. And to the fatherland was due *the first* piece: therefore, pending an answer, this quandary reverberated throughout the following and more easily located deliveries as well. My mother sang, and I ruminated. The fatherland . . . Who knows what it would then do, the incorporeal fatherland, with that piece of Captain's body; not to mention what the others would do with their own embarrassing chunks—maybe a funeral pyre, maybe a burial; maybe someone, his mother at least, would unwrap the bloody bundle and squeeze the piece to her breast. I reflected most of all on the company: all those

Alpine soldiers arranged in a circle around their piece, no one knowing what to say, all of them waiting in silence for a sign from the lieutenant, the lieutenant who says, Don't look at me, it belongs equally to all of us, even to the mules—the gunner Toson turns around and sees that it's true, surrounding the circle of men is a wider circle of mules.

These many mental flights, however, were only the preamble to a more morbid and magnetic investigative torment, which concerned the dual necessity of specifying those pieces as precise anatomic portions, and of pairing them with their respective recipients. That the Captain, in dictating his final will and testament, had his mind made up with clear intentions did not seem a point on which one could cast doubt. I attributed the vagueness of the song to aesthetic convention, while assuming that in reality—even if it was an imaginary reality—everything had been laid out in a more explicit and detailed fashion. And the words of the song themselves, in establishing a sequence, did they not perhaps suggest a plausible distribution of the body parts? The first piece would be the head; the second piece, the shoulders and arms; the third piece, the chest; the fourth piece, the lower abdomen and groin; the last piece, the legs and feet . . . This schema was particularly satisfying for the symbolic congruence between the mountains and the very limbs employed for walking; between the mother and the heart concealed within the chest; between the company and the arms that salute and dole out orders. On the other hand, I wasn't so convinced by the bequests to the beloved and to the fatherland: in terms of the former, there was the intimate vulgarity of those organs, which I did not suspect of having any function other than the discharge of human waste; in the case of the latter, there was the disproportionality between the inestimable gift of the brain and the fatherland itself, which of the five beneficiaries was surely the one to which I would have wanted to see assigned the least precious part.

Thus began a complex process of combination, one that was doomed to end in continual dissatisfaction. The head with the brain, the loving brain, along with the eyes, the contemplative eyes, and with the mouth, the kissing mouth, would go to the beloved; the arms of the faithful servant and soldier, meanwhile, would go to the fatherland; but after confirming the bestowal of the legs to the mountains and the heart to the mother, the groin was left with the Company: that most shameful piece, given to all those people! Exhibited like that, in public! Here, ignited by my own inner protest, a revolutionary intuition took shape: precisely because it was shameful, that piece needed to stay in the family, with the person who, having washed it so many times and, even earlier, having created it, was the only one who could neutralize its unseemliness (and was there not, perhaps, in the attached abdomen the belly button, the maternal navel?). This freed the heart, which, ending up with the beloved, in turn freed the head; and this, as emblem of command (the head of the Captain!), could finally be assigned to the company. But hadn't those Alpini said that they didn't have shoes to walk in? And wasn't *with shoes or without shoes* the most moving moment in that first verse? Well then, why not imagine that in a final flare of solidarity, the Captain wanted to represent to them his will to march forever by their side? If so, the legs and the feet, those bandages wrapped up to the calf, those lumpy, unnailed, mud-encrusted boots, would go to the company and not to the mountains: to which, in exchange, would go—even better than the head (now restored to the beloved)—the heart, the loving heart to his cherished mountains, for it to bloom there with flowers and roses.

And yet something, in this design, still didn't feel right to me. For one, I was aware of having privileged some elements at the expense of others: Why, for instance, did the chest have to be limited to the Captain's heart? Was there not also the breastbone in the chest, the heroic breast that comes between enemy fire and the fatherland, and on which medals are pinned? And what about the hands, the industrious yet caressing hands? And what about the neck? And the back? And, then again, what if the Captain had intended to be sliced in vertical strips or radial, wedgelike sections? The more I became mired in these questions, the more I felt that I was degrading the song's sweetly monstrous charm through my nitpicking—but nevertheless I knew, too, that the very nature of that charm demanded of me a childishly naïve devotion, and naïveté meant, for me, the refusal of any ambiguity.

When the army surgeons undressed the Captain's mortal remains in order to proceed with sectioning, they uncovered a nameless thing, cocooned in a fibrous shell that approximately reproduced the human form. Freed from that simulacrum, the thing expanded like a soaked sponge; then, crackling, it projected glomeruli, mimicked mucus, became burbling raspberry. A line, which looked traced with lipstick, reticulated the amorphous omentum in five areas, each of which had been numbered with didactic foresight from one to

115

five. The surgeons said that, besides the numbers, there was nothing to distinguish any single portion from the others. They said that there was nothing there to see, and they sent away the disturbed troop. Then they cut.

And the company had its piece, but the mountains and the fatherland were far away, on a planet in the system of Cassiopeia: up there, in a pearl-colored valley, a mother and a bride scream out their grief, and I, in certain nights, hear them, and think of Hecuba and Andromache, and say, barren land of Troy left sacked, land of Troy turned to glass, land loved ever more as time has passed, after light years and light years of railroad tracks.

AND I AM THY DAEMON

He was magnificent and proud, but nestled in his gaze was the fragility of distress. He had black skin and barbarous earrings, and a golden cape and the face of Orson Welles. He walked ahead of me, taking long strides down a deserted path in that cemetery, and I nearly had to run to keep up with him. He stopped short upon reaching a grave and, grabbing me by the shoulders, forced me to look at it.

"Now do you believe me?"

On the white marble, the bronze letters spelled out the name of Alessio Baldini, born 1955, died 1965. He had been my classmate in middle school, for the academic years of 1965–66, 1966–67, and 1967–68.

"Impossible," I said. "It must be someone with the same name."

"I'm telling you, it's him."

"Come on now, you think I wouldn't remember Baldini? If only he had died so early!"

"You see? You still haven't gotten over it. Of course you remember, because at the end of that first year he started to play the clown for the sake of a certain Eleonora Merguglia, who had become lord and mistress of your daydreaming medullae, and the more he played the clown the more she delighted in his antics. And so, one morning, during an in-class geometry assignment, you formulated with intensity this thought: 'Oh, how nice, how incredibly nice it would be if Baldini wasn't in class 1F; if on the first day of school something had happened to him instead, something *definitive*'—didn't you think it? And I heard you, I heard the frightening magnitude of your pain and the frightening magnitude of your desire, and I approved."

"Fine, I did think it, but that doesn't change anything."

"You're mistaken, because *I came*."

"And when was this?"

"When you wished that I had. On October 1, 1965, at eight in the morning. I waited for your little friend at the intersection of Via Stendhal and Via Savona, and when he passed by me, I whispered: 'Die.' And, submissively, his *animula parvula* flowed out of him along with his breath and dissipated into the gray air. What remained was his simulacrum, which arrived at school two minutes after the first bell."

"Which means my classmate . . ."

"Was no longer anything at all, mere arid mortal remains, an *exterior*, you understand, nothing more than an empty shell into which you, day after day, for years, continued to pour useless hate. You imagined him enjoying oceans of satisfaction while humming an interminable inner *tra la la*, but you were suffering for nothing, because Baldini was down with me in the icy abyss, and I was squeezing him nice and close to me. And you want to know something else you'll like? He was *screaming*. Even now he hasn't stopped screaming."

"Now?"

"By all appearances he's an insurance broker, but obviously that doesn't mean a thing. The real one is down there, like De Min."

He pushed me in front of another headstone. Maurizio De Min, known as Holden, a boy whose entire existence had revolved around his vulgar motorbike, who talked ceaselessly of Salinger and Bukowski while I read Plutarch and Cervantes in silence, the boy who always wore a mocking or knowing smile . . . that horror of a boy, it said, had passed away "before his time"—ah, but not a moment too soon—on May 7, 1973.

"You remember, don't you? That awful May 6, when during an assembly you found out—yes, under the rumbling of the megaphone you picked up the faintest snippet of a conversation between this De Min character and Ginetta Màngano—you found out that the next day the two of them, just the two of them, would go cruising together, that's how the philistine expressed himself, cruising together for a whole weekend. That night, seeing you so thoroughly tormented by your own imagination, I knew you to be my blood brother, and I decided to help you once again. Your thoughts were so rattled that you couldn't even manage to articulate a precise wish, but the obsessive frequency with which you connected your thirst for blood with that bike spoke volumes . . . "

"I could see them, actually *see* them as they disappeared behind a bend in the road; then I was so incapacitated I couldn't imagine further: only that scene repeated endlessly, the bike slowing down, tilting, and then darting out of view, a continuous dismemberment . . . "

"He listened, bureaucratically, to the Doors while you were moved by Sergio Endrigo, he smoked exotic cigarillos while you munched on mint cough drops, he did and said the things that everyone did and said simply because everyone did and said them, while you legitimately did not understand, could never understand how that conformity could earn him or anyone else the supreme prize of amorous beatitude. That's what I liked about your pain, your complete astonishment, knowing that something is possible or had been possible without ceasing to consider it impossible, that terrible desire *not to be able to believe*, that perpetual absence of peace of mind, your inability to get used to pain, chalking it all up to nature or history . . . You were a passionate reader of Poe, and so at three in the afternoon on that Saturday, May 7, I was there, at the bend in the road, I waited for them to fly past me, and a second before they disappeared behind the curve, I said: 'So long, Toby Dammit.' Three kilometers ahead, a steel cable, inexplicably taut above that freeway at a height of a hundred and sixty centimeters, decapitated him with such a clean slice that his head remained propped up on his neck; being much shorter than him, the girl lost, and just barely, a lock of her splendid hair. That weekend, nothing of what you feared happened, because what did happen was lived out by a dead person. Why are you crying? A dead person, I said, one who couldn't feel anything, understand anything, find pleasure in anything, and all around his neck, right here, remained the red line where he was cut, *swish*. That Monday, you shouldn't have seen him as the most fortunate creature on the face of the earth, for he *was* earth, a golem of unfeeling clay. I tried to tell you but your dreams wouldn't let me in, there were no cracks in your anguish, you spent your youth hating corpses, but know that from that day on no one was spared, not one. Look, over there, Donato Francia, look when he died, Mariano Sampaolo, the horrid Sampaolo, and look there, Walter Sinagra, Marco Podestà, yes, dear old Marchino, what a slab, what stones! Stefano D'Arroglio, Alessandro Tavana—I had him die a truly awful death, you want to know how I made him die?"

I wanted to know, and he told me.

"To those who beat you up, on the other hand, I never did a thing."

"Seems fair."

"To those who stole from you, offended you, wished you harm: not a thing."

"Fair."

"Between the most heinous butcher and Baldini, you would have condemned Baldini every time."

"Yes."

"For those thirteen little smirks, for those twelve wisecracks."

"Yes."

"So, whose wishes was I to grant, if not yours? But you never reaped the benefits."

"How could I, if I lived every moment as if they were alive?"

"But you were the one living out those stories. You were the author and the protagonist of those conversations, of those skipped heartbeats, of all those grazing hands and transcendent entanglements. At least *now* you might consider feeling some relief. Please, a little relief is all I ask!"

"Stories that were lived in their name . . . That's all that counts, *in their name* . . . And, in fact, I've now been struck by a horrifying suspicion: that I was so good at putting myself in my enemies' shoes and gaining an intolerably exact notion of their pleasure precisely for the vacantness of their heads; that in emptying them of life, you got them ready for me like hotel rooms into which I'd free my nightmares . . . To be inside the head of Mariano Sampaolo and look at Rossana Malvezzi *as he would have looked at her*, with *his* drooling, from the perspective of *his* desk, through *his* glasses, and then, on top of all my abdication, you have to add the shame of how zealously I'd fabricate for him a tingle of delight that was all his own, Sampaolo's delight, which was different from D'Arroglio's delight, which was different from Tavana's, because to each, according to his characteristics, I assigned special forms of gratification: if one seemed to fly into ecstasy over blushing shyness, then for him I'd become a novelist of allusions and subtext; if another found pleasure in publicly parading his relationship, I'd hone the cataloguing of outward signs and the whole world became as plain as day; if the face—the skin!—of another suggested melodramatic fevers of a stuttering euphoria, I like a demon sucked the warmth of such hot-blooded passion from the veins of the earth and granted it all to him: then I'd think of him as Mr. Euphoric, and when I was close to going crazy, I'd desperately look for reasons that might take a little of that euphoria away from him, but I wouldn't find any."

"And so you'd go crazy."

"Yes, I'd go crazy every time."

I left him to wander among the graves, looking for some impossible consolation in those slabs of marble.

"Don't you think you're being a tad ungrateful?" he shouted, but a strong wind suddenly rose up and began to carry his words away. Breathlessly, I ran down the path until I came to a portico shielding high walls crammed with burial cells. There, too, semi-hidden by plastic chrysanthemums, the names of my rivals flickered in the light of a few candles. In those cold ashes, there still burned something unbearable, something that would never be restored. I collapsed into a gardener's wheelbarrow. Soon after, I heard his steps echoing loudly under the portico.

"What more could I have done for you?" he asked, with infinite sorrow in his voice. Before answering him, I eased farther down into the wheelbarrow until I felt its icy iron rim on the nape of my neck.

"You could have taken *me*, before I knew desire. At the forming of the first embryo of heartache on account of the back of a knee, where those paper-thin bluish veins are; at the first faintness of breath for a honey-colored braid tied with a black velvet ribbon; at the first and not yet understood feeling of disquiet, away with me! Backtracking that small distance to when there were only tiny toy soldiers and figurines, toy cars, teddies, trading cards, comic booklets, and then clasp me in your clutches there, there among tiny toys and diminutive suffixes, still safe, safe forever—though allowing me to take along just a couple of those little playthings, like an ancient Egyptian, for company."

"This is what you want?"

"I believe it is."

*

One afternoon in April 1963, on the banks of the Rio Lobo, the Union soldier Cooper was fatally shot by the rebel Benson. It was the last shot of my life, after which those toy soldiers, in addition to a Paride Tumburus trading card, an issue of *The Cossack Cocco Bill*, and a Mercury Dauphine model car, vanished into thin air along with me.

DOWN THERE

One summer night in 2030, in the garden of a nursing home, two old men began remembering.

As a little boy I thought that dried apricots were ears, and I'd wonder who the unlucky souls were who'd had them chopped off. When I was forced to try one, picking it up out of a Christmas arrangement of dates and candied fruit, I said to myself, "So this is what ears taste like."

I, on the other hand, believed in a magic powder that, when dissolved in water and drunk, would protect me from bad dreams; and I used to drink it without ever doubting its efficacy. After many years, when I finally asked my mother to show it to me, she replied that once the powder was seen in its natural state it lost its power. I never asked about it again.

I had a father who would stick over his eye a ceramic sphere that perfectly replicated an eyeball: he'd come to me and he'd pretend to pluck his eye out before placing the sphere in his pocket. I'd run away shouting, "Not the eye! Not the eye!"

And I had a father who with a slight incision could remove an orange peel while still leaving it whole. He'd then cut that peel to look like a monstrous mask and, with all the lights off, place a lit candle stub inside it. Looking with dismay at its terrible countenance, I'd hear a cavernous voice saying, "Behold, I am The Face, and I have come for you."

I had a grandfather who one day told me the story of Henry VIII, who murdered all of his wives. Instead of the "the eighth," however, I heard "tea ate," and for many years, every time I accidentally swallowed any bits of leaves at the bottom of my mug of tea, I'd wait to recognize the first symptoms of poisoning.

I, too, had a grandfather, who one Sunday took me to San Siro to see my first soccer match. During halftime he explained to me that AC Milan wasn't able to score because Fiorentina had Robotti. I took it to mean "robots," and I spent the second half trying to discern a mechanical quality in the movements of the purple players. Coming home, it seemed like nothing short of a miracle if the game had ended zero–zero, with us up against indestructible steel!

Well, whenever I swam out past the buoy, I always expected to get torn to bits by a shark or dogfish. I thus ruined ten years of swimming, until the day I figured out that all I needed to do was stick my head under water and say, "Wherever you are, know that I am a fish like you."

Meanwhile, whenever I was by the seashore, I'd be terrified that the hook of a distracted fisherman might poke through my eye, or my tongue, or an ear, and tear them right out like bait for the fishes.

I had a father who used to take me to see the church of San Bernardino alle Ossa, and the Fopponino chapel full of skulls with a Latin inscription that could be translated as "Do not deride us, passer-by, because one day you will be as us." I would look at them awhile and think, "Not me, no deriding here."

Mine sent me a postcard of the Capuchin Crypt from Palermo, and from Turin a photograph of a mummy in the Egyptian Museum. Seeing them in my room, my grandmother exclaimed, "Are these things to show to little boys?" And on the inside, I said, "Apparently, they are."

One of the very first times I made a phone call, I convinced myself that if no one picked up, it maybe meant they were dead. From that moment on, for my whole life, I haven't been able to get to the third ring without thinking, "Something terrible must have happened."

As for me, when I had grown up a bit and saw *The Exorcist*, *The Thing*, *The Evil Dead*, *Jaws*, and *Alien*, I didn't see anything that wasn't already familiar—extremely familiar, going back as far as I could remember.

I was convinced that everything that was visible—people, cars, swallows, power lines, spit on the sidewalk—was a performance staged around me in order to study my behavior. Feeling observed, I acted so as to never let on that I'd figured it all out: an aware guinea pig, I told myself, is a useless guinea pig, meaning a guinea pig to be eliminated.

Whereas when someone would smile at me too affectionately, I'd get the suspicion that they weren't real: the Fake Mother, the Fake Uncle, the Fake Stationer. And along with terror, I'd feel great sorrow over the fate of the originals.

I once went to the movies with my parents to see *Vampyr* by Dreyer. At the last second, thinking that it would scare me too much, they opted for Rossellini's *The White Ship* instead. I didn't notice the switch, so throughout the whole film I waited in vain for the monster to appear. For days afterward I beat myself up for having failed to recognize him among all those sailors.

I had a grandfather who used to make hundreds of little nude women out of clay. He based the bodily proportions on the Canon of Polykleitos, but since he had written down one of the measurements incorrectly, all of the women ended up with their legs too short and their butts too low. Looking at those butts, he'd sigh dejectedly, and if my father or my uncle suggested he sculpt them a little higher up, he'd reply, "You all think you know more than Polykleitos, do you?" What I understood, then, was that Polykleitos must have been an old enemy of my grandfather's.

Once, when I was too reticent to talk about a certain topic, my father said to me, "You know that everything you're living through now, I already lived through it myself when I was your age—so there's nothing in your mind that I don't know." From that day on, I felt so *evident* in his eyes that every comment or confession became pointless. In this way, my reticence became total.

And once, when I couldn't fall asleep, I got out of bed and secretly went to listen by the door to the room where the adults were chatting. I heard them say names I didn't know, I heard new tones of voice; I understood that my life and theirs were separate things, and it was only by chance that one ever encountered the other during the daytime.

Back in middle school, I would often go to the library to take out books. One day the school librarian made a mistake, and instead of *Troy and Its Remains* by Heinrich Schliemann he accidentally gave me a little volume titled *Death Will Come and Will Have Your Eyes*. There's no sum in the world that could ever compensate me for that mix-up.

I had a nanny who would sleep in my bedroom at our house in the country. After we'd been lying there in the dark for a little while, I'd ask, "Dirce, are you there?" and I'd hear in response: "No, I'm not here." Perplexed, I would point out, "But that was your voice"—to which she'd reply, merciless and poetic at the same time, "I'm not Dirce, I'm a little voice far, far away, coming from the woods . . . " And, knowing and not knowing, believing and not believing, I'd then have to face the night like that, as if it were a test.

My father knew an electrician who had lost his thumb in the hatch of an airplane. When he came to our house for lunch and noticed the effort I was making not to stare, he showed me his intact hand with his thumb hidden behind the other fingers; then he made it suddenly pop back out. He didn't understand that precisely in that manner, by leading me to believe he could do the same with the other hand, he truly became monstrous to me.

When my mother explained to me that "monster" in ancient times meant an omen, or even a miracle, for a second I felt put at ease, as though I were living in a better world.

The fundamental book in my upbringing was *Slovenly Peter*, and since I used to suck my thumb, my greatest nightmare was the Tailor:

> The door opens, the tailor has come,
> Leaping toward him to cut those thumbs.
> He slices through them like a shirt,
> The boy cries out: "Oh no, that hurts!"

Slovenly Peter was my favorite book too, and even if I did eat a lot, I felt awful for poor Kaspar, who wasted away and died because he kept saying, "I don't want it, I said no way, I won't eat any soup today," and on whose grave they laid a soup bowl.

But now, before we go back inside, why don't we talk about something pleasant.

Okay. When he was in a good mood, my father would say to me, "Hey piggy," or "Hey piglet," or "Hey little porker." Left on my own, I'd say to myself, "Yes, I am a piggy," and I would laugh.

When making a snack, I used to fill a bowl of milk with little pieces of bread until the spoon could stay standing in it all on its own. If my father came into the kitchen, he'd say to me, "What a nice mishmash!"—and he'd steal some from my bowl.

There wasn't much else, in life.

No, it's almost all down there.

from

EURYDICE
HAD A DOG

THE SOCCER BALLS
OF MR. KURZ

For Bragonzi, the only beautiful thing in the sad life of the boarding school in Quarto dei Mille were the soccer matches. And yet even that beauty was anguished. He realized it as early as the first match, when he saw that once the moment came to shoot, even the best, even the oldest players suffered a kind of muscular contraction, as if forcing themselves to hold back; and, in fact, what emerged was a weak, uncertain shot, which the goalie blocked with ease. And to think that a second earlier that same forward had seemed full of confident vigor, impetuously swooping down onto the ball, defending it, rushing with long strides toward the goal area—but then . . . but then that feeble shot.

Only at the third match did he make up his mind to ask, after he'd happened to give a hard kick and the ball, flying upward, just barely missed going over to the other side, beyond the wall that constituted the end of the schoolyard: "Aaaah . . ." all the little boys groaned in chorus, covering their eyes with their hands, and when the ball fell back down in the schoolyard, rather than rejoicing, they rebuked Bragonzi bitterly. "But why? What did I do wrong?" he asked Paltonieri as they went back inside for snack time. "And even if the ball did go over, why make such a big deal about it?"

And so Paltonieri explained. He said that on the other side of the wall lived a Mr. Kurz, whom no one had ever seen but who must have hated all of the boarding school children, because whenever the ball ended up on his side he never gave it back (as is civil and urbane custom: you've sent it hurtling over there and now you anxiously wait, speculating by the wall, and lo, by silent miracle it returns, tracing its trajectory in the sky, returning, returning—and with your heart over-flowing with gratitude you give resounding thanks: "Thank you!" you say, you don't know to whom, but you say it. Or else the miracle is delayed, and you walk away uncertainly, saddened by the game's forced end; but when you come back the following morning the ball is there in the yard, for how long you don't know, and so your "thank you" is all the more heartfelt, because you only think it, addressing it to the past). Not only that, but vain would have been any attempt to get the ball back; at least this was what was claimed by the young Instructresses, who, a long time ago, caving to universal insistence, had gone over to speak to Mr. Kurz. "Mr. Kurz is well within his rights," they apparently relayed with an air of annoyance, "and can keep whatever makes its way into his yard." Such a response, noted Paltonieri, who had heard the story from Morchiolini, sent the message that the Instructresses hadn't put much of an effort into their mission: if only the boys could have gone themselves, just once, to speak to that man, maybe they would have convinced him, maybe he would have yelled at them a little, sure, but in the end he would have given back all the balls confiscated that year and, who knows, even previous years. But nothing could be done, the rules barred the boys from leaving the school,

136

and besides, what would be the point? Mr. Kurz had said no to *them*, and they were schoolmistresses—never mind a bunch of snot-nosed kids! For that matter, the Instructresses had added, from that day forward they would not be going back to see that man. They had a sense of dignity, they did, and they weren't interested in being humiliated by someone who—they stressed with a hint of sadism—happened to be correct!

Of course, Paltonieri continued, if the school had been endowed with an ample supply of soccer balls, there would be nothing to get upset about in all this, if they lost one they could requisition another, and Mr. Kurz could do as he pleased. But the reality was that an endowment of balls not only wasn't ample, but wasn't even provided for, and they had to make do with the odd privately owned ball. "Do you understand what this means?" Paltonieri pressed Bragonzi, now thoroughly worked up. "It means having to keep tabs on the new kids, the ones who've just arrived with a suitcase full of toys, and hope that they have a ball, and if they do, convince them to lend it to us, giving them gifts, which is already enough to make them suspicious, maybe the ball is new and so they guard it jealously, and if you try to take it away from them they squeal and then the Instructresses come running, understand? And when you've finally convinced them—you've given them heaps of trading cards and comics, promised them they'll also get to play, even if they're so little they don't have a clue what a soccer match is—when finally it's all worked out and the game begins, *pow!* some idiot kicks the ball over the wall, and we're ruined. And it's not even possible to get our parents to buy balls when they come to see us and take us to Genoa, because visiting days are on Sunday and everything's closed . . . You know today's ball, the one you almost sent over to the other side? It's Randazzo's, and to get it he had to write to his dad a month ago, telling him to bring it last Friday, and his dad lives in Messina and only comes twice a year, understand?"

Bragonzi understood, and he understood, too, that theirs would never be real matches, but monstrosities, unnerving endeavors in which, more than the struggle between the two teams, what counted was the unspoken battle being played between all of them and that cruel man lying in wait. As months passed, this image grew and grew in Bragonzi's mind, while he became accustomed to thinking of Mr. Kurz as an enormous black spider, motionless in the middle of his yard but lightning-fast when pouncing on the balls that fell like fat insects into his web: then, seizing them with his foul legs, horrifically he sucked till there was naught left but the floppy remains . . . This rapacity was the scariest thing of all, because it wrapped around and bound up the soccer ball even before it went over the wall, calling it and infecting it with a bluish leprosy, so that playing with it was a bit like contracting that disease, or like conversing with a man condemned to death; other times, rather, it seemed to him that the ball was a beautiful woman promised in marriage to a jealous tyrant, and that horrible torments awaited the reckless fool who dared so much as to graze her.

It was but little consolation that he now played on a permanent basis for the Weenies. Dividing all the boys into Champs and Weenies had been thought up by Saniosi, whose intellect, faced with the impossibility of resolving the problem of Mr. Kurz, had at least conceived of a way to transform that nightmarish presence from a paralyzing element into an active part of the game. What he proposed was simple, and founded on the eradication of switching sides at halftime: the Weenies would always shoot at the goal chalked on the dormitory wall, the Champs at the one on the wall separating the schoolyard from Mr. Kurz; that way, Saniosi thought, the fear of losing the ball would hinder the Champs, weakening their abilities and thus leveling the playing field. And so it was—but for the fact that everyone wanted to be welcomed into the ranks of the Weenies, and to this end deliberately tripped themselves up, displayed profound shortcomings in technique never previously revealed, spread their legs wide open so as to garner the supreme humiliation of the nutmeg. It became necessary to form a tribunal of memory-keepers, who by punctiliously citing dribbling and counterattacks, crosses and headed goals, forced the Champs to face, with no chance of appeal, their own talent.

So Bragonzi was a Weenie, but this didn't prevent him from sensing during the games—almost absorbing it from the uncertain looks in the eyes of the Champs—a general sense of distress. This feeling only worsened after the episode with Lamorchia.

It happened as follows: For an excruciatingly long week, the boys were left without a ball, to rave, bored, in the emptiness. Then, on Sunday, Tabidini's dad took his son to Genoa. Seeing him heave a sigh in front of the lowered shutter of a toy store, he questioned the boy and, finding out the truth, gave a good long laugh; then, without another word, he took his son by the hand and pulled him along until they reached the nearest park, where several gangs of children were playing ball. "Which would you like?" he asked, encompassing in a single wave of his hand that entire swarm.

"What do you mean, 'which'?" gulped Tabidini, who had understood perfectly.

"Don't you worry about it. There must be a ball here that tickles your fancy more than the others, no?"

Tabidini observed: over here the children were gratifying themselves with an unsizable rubber sphere, colorful and flabby, the kind for little kids; another group, right behind them, was scrambling around a ball that was more serious but also deflated—you could tell from the noise it made and from its pitiful bounce. Tabidini looked beyond the drinking fountain: over there was the biggest showdown, with at least ten players per side, and the ball was sound, but lightweight too, made of taut plastic, one of those balls that shoot up bizarrely, almost taking flight of their own volition, no, no, too dangerous, a real shame though; to their left, in a completely grassless area, enshrouded in an earthy cloud, six desperately lanky dawdlers were playing with a dirt-colored ball of an indecipherable nature—he looked at them more closely: they didn't have "the goods" and were playing in loafers, their long socks pulled up to their knees, a scraping of soles, a slip-sliding amid expletives. Tabidini waited for the ball to emerge for an instant from the dust cloud to observe it more carefully: huh, it was leather, one of those prehistoric hand-stitched balls, with a wide valve like a ten-lire coin and that nutty color that had been vanquished long ago by black-and-white: weighty and lumpy and somewhat pear-shaped, of a mineral substance that had been chemically enriched over the years with mud and emotions . . . headaches and blackened nails lay in store for the imprudent soul who opted for that ball, no thank you, better take a look at that other group in the field all the way at the far end; he asked his father for permission to go, then walked through the park until he was close enough to taste this new match: a match into which fathers and sisters had been frivolously mixed, a match that was revolving, alas, around an exceedingly light beach ball, literally lighter than a feather, a complimentary item included with the purchase of sunscreen for the sportily benighted. Disheartened, Tabidini went back to his dad, with one last glance at some other pilgrims who were blissfully delighting, poor fools! in a felt tennis ball.

"Well then?"

Tabidini was about to reply that he wasn't exactly spoiled for choice when he was distracted by the simultaneous arrival of four cars, then of two more right after. Out of them came twenty or so older adolescents in tracksuits, loaded with gym bags and duffel bags; it was enough for one of them to tweak his hamstring muscles, tenderizing them a bit, for Tabidini, melting with emotion, to understand: yes, he didn't need to see over it to know what was behind the park's high gray wall, the group's clear destination. A real soccer field! A real match! he thought, now liquefied, just as one of the last adolescents, having rested his duffel on the ground, pulled out a plastic bag, which he opened and then put back down, laying bare its contents: shimmering in the morning light of the sun, so new and untouched as to appear enameled, flawlessly round, soft and taut at once, planet of glory, the most beautiful soccer ball Tabidini had ever seen. Propelled by an irrepressible impulse, he slipped his chubby hand out of his father's and started to run toward the player, who had remained behind his companions and was now meticulously closing his duffel bag. As soon as he was close enough to make out the words, Tabidini stopped, and he read: "World Cup." Oh! His heart skipped a beat. And then, right below, in a different pentagon: "Official Soccer Ball—Patented—Licensed—Tested," and slightly lower still: "No. 3." But what made Tabidini's eyes bulge out of his head was the signature, the fluttering signature stamped along the length of two other pentagons (at first glance he didn't want to believe it, looked more closely at the squiggle—but yes, it was true, beyond a shadow of a doubt): "George Best." Best! Best's soccer ball! The greatest player of them all! The legend who was invoked after every intoxicating mazy run! At school, they'd only ever had one ball with a name on it to date: "Totonno Juliano," it was called, it even bore his picture, though the product was made of plastic, brought back from Naples by Fiorillo: a good ball, but nothing more, and in any event, after just a few days it became the prey of Mr. Kurz. But this one! And Best's to boot! Desperately he turned toward his father, who started to walk over. Meanwhile, the adolescent, giving a shout to his companions, sent the ball their way, essentially inviting them to have a taste. Tabidini was no stranger to that weakness, that yielding to the temptation to try out a new ball while still off the field and out in the street, despite knowing full well that the rough concrete would leave a mark on its luster—as if the owner, unable to bear so much perfection, wanted to artificially dirty and age the ball in order to finally recognize it as his own.

Mr. Tabidini knew his son. Without saying a word, he trotted over to the youngsters, whom he reached right at the little iron gateway in the wall. At a distance, his son watched them talk: his father on one side, the others curved around in a semicircle, their bags placed on the ground. They were shaking their heads, gesticulating nervously. Then his father took his wallet out of his jacket and started sliding out bills. The players shook their heads some more; then, seeing as he was still pulling out bills, they started to discuss the matter among themselves. One of them moved off, gesturing as if to tell another to go to hell, then he came back. Now Tabidini's dad was standing there in silence; one guy came right up to him shaking his fists, but three others grabbed him and shoved him out of the group. The discussion continued until Tabidini's father finally stuck his fingers back into his wallet. When Tabidini saw one of the players pick the ball up and hand it to his father, he thought he was dreaming. Kissed by the sun as he walked back over to him (the adolescents, behind, went on gesticulating and arguing), Tabidini's father looked like a paladin returning with the Grail.

That evening, in a jubilant riot of ooohs and aaahs, Tabidini was greeted by the entire boarding school as a hero, and every boy, before falling asleep, fantasized in his bed about the match announced for the following day. So radiant was the image of George Best that, for one night, there was no room in their heads for Mr. Kurz.

What followed was something horrific, and each boy found himself suddenly older. Bragonzi was left with the special sorrow of having failed to touch the ball even once. It was only a minute into the game, the Champs were on the attack, when the ball rebounded and went soaring into the air like a sublime bird: in everyone's consciousness it came back down in slow motion, while below a roaring, elbowing melee raged. In the general confusion, no one noticed Lamorchia—only Bragonzi saw him getting ready to kick a volley: "No! No!" he shouted, or maybe he merely thought it, while the ball descended with unreal slowness, and already that kid was slanting, twisting his upper body and rearing back his right leg, already he was bending his knee as he lifted his shoe off the ground, "No! No!" not like this, not in the air, let it bounce, but Lamorchia couldn't hear him, it was as though he was being drawn heavenward, ankle first, every sensory faculty now transferred to that ascending ankle, into that outward thrust that is called an instep. Abandoning the man he was marking, Bragonzi dived into the melee toward Lamorchia, imploring him all the while, sending him messages, and then, in a flash, everyone realized, and froze as if turned to stone, their limbs caught and tangled, and, unable to give voice, each one thought inside himself *Don't do it, don't do it*, no one daring to look at Lamorchia's ankle, only looking at his swooning eye, captivated by his bliss and at the same time horrified . . . *pow!* went the ball as it was struck from too low and from the side, rising once again, though no longer vertically, rather in an excruciating, mournful trajectory: Best's soccer ball fell precisely on the flat top of the wall, taking everyone's breath away, and then, after an imperceptible stasis, it plunged down definitively on the other side, and became the property of Mr. Kurz.

No one did Lamorchia any harm, because the harm was locked in their hearts. Lamorchia himself, for that matter, was never the same after that day, nor did he ever again wish to play soccer: he could be seen off at the edge of the field, sitting like a pensioner warming himself in the afternoon sun, and when the ball wound up in his vicinity, and shouts of "Ball!" were directed at him from the field, he would pick it up, but, not having the courage to kick or throw it, he would carry it all the way to the center of the field, squeezing it to his chest, and, once there, set it down with care.

Six months had passed since that day, during which at least twelve balls had made their way to Mr. Kurz; then, tired of so much heartache, they ceased to play except with balls of knotted rags, which had the advantage of never leaving the ground: monstrous turbans that kept up the fiction of sphericality for no more than half an hour before starting to unravel, coarse comets dragging a tail of dusty tatters. After four months of this punishing humiliation, Bragonzi stopped one fine fall day in the middle of a rightward attack, and amid general protest grabbed with his hands that simulacrum of a ball.

"Companions, friends," he would have said if he had been an ancient tribune, "consider who we are, who we have been, and, gazing upon yourselves in this ignominious rag as in a mirror, may you hence derive sufficient shame to spur you to redeem a life perhaps not yet lost to the cause of Soccer. Think of those who, scorning danger, preceded us on this selfsame field, and let it conjure within you those Greats in whose shadow all of us, in regrettably distant days of yore, sought to shape ourselves, Tumburus, Fogli, Mora, Pascutti, Bobby Charlton, Chinesinho, Del Sol: they are watching us—and do we not shudder? And yet we hesitate?"

His words were not these, naturally, but this was the spirit, and the result—judging by the gritting of teeth—was no different from the one such a speech would have inspired. And so war was declared, but for the moment, needing also to fight on the internal front with the Instructresses, and not knowing what they would find on the other side of the wall, they limited their actions to the launching of a reconnaissance mission. In the insanity of the hour, everyone volunteered, but it was unanimously decided that if there was one among their number to whom the honor of that mission was rightfully owed, it was Bragonzi. To decide who would join him, they proceeded to draw lots, from which emerged the names of Tabidini and Sieroni.

At two o'clock that night, Bragonzi slid out from under his covers and, feeling his way along the walls in the dark, came to the end of the hallway, where their assigned Instructress's bedroom lay. He knocked three times, and when she opened the door, disheveled and furious and searching in the shadows for whoever the pest was, he said in one breath, "Quick, come, Tabidini is unwell!" While she ran to the afflicted, though not before covering her shoulders with a bed shawl, Bragonzi infiltrated her room and rummaged through everything (resisting the distraction of stockings and laces) until he found the coveted bunch of keys. Then, after hiding them in a carefully selected spot in the bathroom, he went back into the dormitory, giving the agreed-upon signal to Tabidini, who promptly ceased his stertorous gurgling.

An hour later, when silence reigned anew, Bragonzi and Sieroni got dressed and slipped like thieves from their beds to the bathroom, and, with the keys retrieved, were now masters of the boarding school. First, they opened the janitor's closet, grabbing a flashlight and a handsome collection of different screwdrivers; then, after unlocking two other doors, they exited onto the field, and suddenly (or was it only a shiver from the freezing air?) it was as though Mr. Kurz could see them. One last door, to the gardener's shed, and they came into possession of a long ladder. Bragonzi tried his best not to think about what he was doing, and, actually, thanks to a hint of fever, he was aware of it all as though he were already remembering it, as though it were a thing of the past: the ladder, which was slightly shorter than the wall; the struggle to stand it upright like an Egyptian obelisk; Sieroni hesitating due to an onset of second thoughts which resulted in a necessary rebuke; his own frightening ascent, rung after rung, with the terror of spotting over the top of the wall the first of the eight hairy legs; his precarious balancing act up at the top followed by the work of lifting the ladder and lowering it on the other side, first pushed from below by Sieroni, then held solely with his own strength, the cold air on his face and the impossibility of seeing anything whatever on Mr. Kurz's side, Sieroni's whimpering invitation to turn back, and, at last, his descent into the darkness below.

After landing in Kurz's yard, Bragonzi stood a long while in silence, until, all being quiet, he finally turned on the flashlight. The yard was small, much smaller than theirs, and not paved. Here, then, on this earth, was where the balls fell. In front of him, a low house, two stories, its windows shut: Kurz's house. On its sides, the yard ended at two walls that were as tall as the one he had just climbed, but along the left wall ran a strange, glimmering structure. Bragonzi approached it and saw that it was made of glass, with leaded panes: Kurz's greenhouse. He tried to look inside, but the glass offered back only the flashlight's glow. The perfect place to hide the ladder, he thought, for if Kurz sees it I'm a goner. His next thought was that the screwdrivers would now come in handy, but there was no need for them: the little door was closed by a latch with no padlock, and that things could be so easy immediately brought back to mind the ghastly mouth of the spider.

Having flung the door wide, he dragged and then pushed the ladder inside, making sure to erase the grooves left on the ground: he had seen this done in movies by American Indian women to the tracks of their shining warriors. Now that he was shut inside the greenhouse, he turned the flashlight back on in order to better conceal the ladder, and he saw them. He saw all of them, all at once, and with them, the generations, the jerseys, the hopes, the dashes and dives.

The greenhouse was filled with three long shelving units, two units on the sides and one in the center, like a kind of backbone, resulting in two parallel corridors; each had seven rows of shelves, each row a continuous line of flowerpots, each pot holding a soccer ball. Slightly larger in diameter than the pots, the balls protruded by three fourths, touching one another at the sides like the segments of a monstrous caterpillar. Stunned, unsure whether to be horrified or to rejoice, his heart rioting in his chest, Bragonzi moved closer and focused the beam of light on the first ball on the shelf to his left. It was an incredibly old ball, more gray than brown, completely peeled and with several unstitched seams; he touched it: the coarsest thing he had ever felt. There was something written on the pot in black block letters, faded with time: "May 8, 1933." Bragonzi was trembling. He lit the next ball: this one looked worn out like an old sweater and, busted, dented, and covered in stains resembling tar, it sank deeper than the others into its pot; for this one, too, the pot bore a faded inscription: "November 13, 1933." It's a dream, Bragonzi thought, refusing to understand. He slowly went down the corridor, moving the beam of light: February 4, 1934, April 28, 1934, May 16, 1934, June 2, 1934, June 18, 1934, August 3, 1934, September 3, 1934 . . . then eight balls from 1935, six from 1936, ten from 1937, seven from 1938, five from 1939, none from 1940 to 1945, twelve from 1946, sixteen from 1947 . . . Could it be? He turned from the shelves on the left, and pointing the light at the central unit, immediately read: "July 21, 1956." This one was a double shelf, each pot corresponding to another pot facing the opposite side; here he ran breathlessly, and read at random: "March 7, 1960," "August 11, 1961." And, finally, the shelves on the right, full of orbs from 1963, from '64, from '65, from '66 . . . Overcome, he sped up his pace as he moved down the aisle, toward the back, where he knew what he would find . . . He would find Fermenti's soccer ball, the very first one he had seen go flying over to the other—to this—side, and Randazzo's ball, there they were! and the "Totonno Juliano" (there! "March 9, 1967," yes, that was the day it happened), and his own, his red-and-black beloved, it was there too (he was about to take it, but withdrew his hand), and all the others up to Best's, there it was! shining more brightly than the rest in the glow of the flashlight, still unblemished and new-smelling, and then all the lost balls up to the day of their conversion to

149

rags, not one was missing, oh, dearest soccer balls! But what sent a shudder running through his entire body was what he saw *after* the last ball, even if he could have imagined it beforehand: a line of empty pots, ready to welcome the new arrivals . . .

He contemplated at length the emptiness of those pots, successively lighting up their interiors, and he wondered where, in that precise moment, the balls destined to fill them were, in what storeroom or window display, and wondered, too, when they would rain down like ripe fruits from over the wall, on what date, a sixteenth of October or a twentieth of March—impossible to say. For now, the boys played with balls made of rags, but someday things would go back to normal, it was inevitable, and on that day, Mr. Kurz would be happy once more. What did he think of that temporary suspension of soccer balls? Maybe from the more muffled sound of their kicks he had figured out the truth and was awaiting his hour, as he had since 1933 . . . Bragonzi returned to the front of the greenhouse and stood before that first ball: looking at it, and thinking that those who had played with it must be older than his father by now, he considered how the balls with which an individual plays in his life get lost in thousands of ways, rolling down countless streets, ending up in rivers and on rooftops, torn apart by the teeth of dogs or boiled by the sun, deflating like shriveled prunes or exploding on the pikes of gates, or simply disappearing, you thought you had them and you look all over but they're nowhere to be found, who knows how much time has passed since you lost them or since someone swiped them at the park; he considered how all of the balls touched by those children had thus dissipated, and if he were in their presence and asked them, "Where are all of your soccer balls?" they would shrug, unable to account for the fate of a single one. Only that ball had been snatched from the clutches of destruction, only that ball, from May 9, 1933, went on being a ball. Oh, he knew all too well how things had unfolded, how many times had he witnessed the same scene! The ball had shot upward, and even before it went over the wall, everyone thought, "It's lost—goodbye, ball." But no, only in that moment was it saved. And many years later, when all those children went down into their graves, that ball would be more alive than them, the last memory of the matches of yesteryear.

Bragonzi passed one more time through the entire collection, observing more closely some spheres that he hadn't noticed before, a hard and clumpy one resembling a truffle, a still pristine one on which was written "From Grandma, to her sweet pea," a rubber one with the faces of the players who died in the Superga air disaster, one with Hamrin's signature forged by an uncertain juvenile hand. And he noticed something else, which brought a lump to his throat: Mr. Kurz had arranged each ball in its pot so as to look its best, the least dented or unstitched part forward, the part with the faces or signatures, as though he loved those soccer balls.

The glow of the flashlight kept growing dimmer, and so Bragonzi decided to turn it off for a little while. In the darkness, after a few seconds had passed, the silhouettes of the soccer balls began to appear like fluorescent specters, first the whiter ones, then slowly but surely the rest, and it seemed to Bragonzi that they were quivering, and that they wanted to say something. Concentrated in that luminescence was the first glimmer of morning, as yet imperceptible in the sky. Before long it would be dawn (had he then been in the greenhouse for that long?), and Bragonzi didn't know what to do, whether to turn the flashlight back on and keep looking around, or get out of there, or scope out other areas of the yard. Instead he carried on as before, wandering slowly up and down those two corridors, one moment laying his hands on an orb whose pentagons looked like black fish in a pitcher of water, the next on a globe of gaseous yellow.

The first light of sunrise took him by surprise and convinced him to go back. He dragged the ladder to the foot of the wall after being assailed by a gust of freezing air upon leaving the greenhouse. Then, right as he was about to climb the ladder, he saw something in the middle of the yard, something that had been hidden, before, in the dark. He moved closer: it was a wooden chair with a wicker seat, turned to face the boarding school. Oh, it didn't take much to understand what the person who would sit in it waited for, and Bragonzi shivered at the thought of him sitting there, motionless, patient, day after day from morning till night, saddened by the fruitless days, weeks, months . . . He immediately walked away from the chair, then he went back; he wanted to try to sit in it, and did. Opposite, one saw only the wall, and above, the sky, nothing more. He tried to imagine a match taking place behind that wall, Secerni's attacks, Saniosi's feints, Piva's fouls, Fognin's drives. He saw the sweaty faces, the dust clouds, the scraped and scabbed knees, he saw the arguments over offsides and the rock paper scissors to decide the teams, he saw the rage and he saw the joy. And he saw a ball spring up from the top of the wall like a black moon from the sea, saw it rise, tracing its arc in the sky, and falling to earth on this side, bouncing a few meters from the chair, then stopping meekly in the dust. Hello, ball, he said, tenderly contemplating it in the light of the dawn.

When he reached the top of the wall, he realized that Sieroni had fallen asleep on the ground, right there below him; he woke him by dropping a shoe on his back. He then pulled up the ladder and climbed back down into the schoolyard. At the first occasion they had to talk about it, his throng of classmates made only a collective impression upon him while—unable to bring any one face or name into focus, surrounded by their disappointed eyes—he told of locked doors and darkness.

It rained the following days, and the schoolyard remained deserted. That Sunday, their Instructress told Bragonzi that there was a surprise in store for him, his dad had come from Milan to see him, he was to run and get dressed, chop chop! His dad took him to a restaurant and then to the movies to see a Lemmy Caution film, after which they strolled around the port looking at the ships. Toward evening they got in a taxi, but instead of giving the school's address, his father said, "To the train station." Bragonzi didn't ask any questions, and he kept silent even in the baggage room, where his father reclaimed a big black bag. They returned to the school in another taxi, and only when they were in front of the gate, with the taxi driver waiting to head back to the station, did his father crouch down and open it. The first thing to emerge was an issue of *Soldino*, but already Bragonzi had started to tremble; then came a stick of modeling clay and a

153

little puzzle, and meanwhile the rustling of cellophane could be heard underneath; then there was a balsa-wood model airplane kit; and then, finally, that transparent bag, which his father gave to him after making him wait longer than for the other presents, as he smiled back in silence and hoped that his tremors weren't visible. "Thank you," he said, and he wanted to add something else, but while he was thinking about what this should be his dad had already gotten back in the taxi. And so Bragonzi hid everything under his raincoat and ran back to the dormitory. It was already past the hour when boys needed to come back from any outings "already fed," for the rules barred these temporary escapees from joining the others in the refectory during meals (his father didn't know this, since he'd never been brave enough to tell him), and so there was no one around. After putting the other presents in his closet, Bragonzi sat on the bed with the see-through bag on his knees. It was closed with a thin red string and, in addition to the ball, contained the pump and the needle for inflating it, as well as a little box of wax and a small felt cloth with zigzag edges for polishing: once opened, the bag released a delightful leathery aroma, which reminded Bragonzi of the smell of his nicest pair of shoes. The pump was icy cold, the ball less so. He stuck the needle into its valve and began to inflate with care: some of the air in this room, he thought, is going to end up inside there, and it will never come out again. When every last pentagon had popped out convexly, he removed the needle. He spread his thighs slightly apart to better hold the ball, not wanting it to touch the floor. It was magnificent, a Derby Star "Deliciae Platearum" even more beautiful than Best's "World Cup" ball; he couldn't imagine how hard his father must have had to look before finding it, or how much he had paid for it, its white just slightly pearlier than the rest, with iridescent reflections, and black pentagons framed by a subtle red outline, and a little yellow star right underneath its brand name, a ball even Rivera would kick cautiously, truly like nothing he had ever seen before . . . He fondled it awhile with his fingertips and slid it against his cheeks to take in all of its smoothness, decided to give it a few more pumps, then went back to caressing it. He looked at the clock: before long they would all be coming back upstairs, he had to be quick. He put the pump and the bag in the closet, and went down to the atrium with the "Deliciae Platearum" under his arm. From there, he passed through the television lounge before skirting the refectory, crouching down beneath the windows so as not to be spotted by the diners; at the end of the hallway, the door to the schoolyard was open—the Instructresses liked to take a stroll right after dinnertime.

It was not yet completely dark in the schoolyard, and from the sky, now that the rain had stopped and the clouds had been torn asunder, Bragonzi could tell that the next day would be a beautiful one. He avoided the puddles as he moved to the center of the soccer field, which was marked with faded white paint. He looked at the ball in his hands, even more beautiful in the moonlight. He checked that the top of his right shoe wasn't muddy, looked at the wall in front of him and then above the wall too, took a deep breath, looked once more at the ball, threw it into the air, waited for it to come back down, and kicked it with his instep when it was roughly thirty centimeters from the ground, and he knew from the sound it made that he had kicked it well, saw it rise quickly into the air, first darkly silhouetted against a cloud whitened by the moonlight, then brightly against the night sky, and it seemed to rest there, suspended in midair, until it descended, and disappeared behind the black horizon of the wall.

Now he could go back, and bury himself in his bed.

EURYDICE HAD A DOG

Scalna was never a town. Scalna ended where the stones of our walkway ended, at that green gate and at the wall that hugged our yard on both sides, extending as far north as the hayloft and the woodshed, and as far south as our house. That was Scalna, that yard and those three structures, and the large vegetable garden that stretched out behind the house, demarcated by the tall wire mesh fencing covered in vines. All that fell outside those confines I did not dignify with a name: it was simply "the town." The maps and the train timetables did not beguile me: yes, they called the whole area "Scalna," but whoever had written that name, I knew, meant to refer fundamentally to our house; and even the arrows in the road signs pointed to nothing other than *that* house, as with a museum or ancient basilica.

We had neighbors, the Baldi family. Their house had one less floor than ours; it was newer and smaller, and uglier too. But that wasn't the reason why, as soon as I'd see them, I felt a sense of commiseration: I believe it was because I knew that they lived—they, like everyone else—in a house that wasn't the real one, that wasn't the right one, and because I knew they were oblivious to their own misery. It seemed unthinkable that they wouldn't at least have an inkling, a sense of exclusion or a touch of envy, yet so it was, and

I received the proof of it the day I bumped into one of them in Milan, Franco, who asked me if I, too, would be going to Scalna at the end of June as I always did. "I, too?" I thought, scandalized. "I will go to Scalna, though I'm not sure about all of you. You'll just get close."

Scalna was where I spent every summer, along with my grandparents and sometimes my sister as well. Summer after summer, never-endingly, from when I was born until just a few years ago, when the destruction of too many trees and too many other things, opening unhealable wounds, rendered permanently mournful my returns, and their memory. But the truth is that things had started to change and the trees to fall much earlier, and it was partly in order to look at my surroundings as little as possible that in later years I hardly ever left the library, where at least everything continued to stay as it was, the yellowed books and the moisture stains on the wall, the pear-colored couch and the telescope in a corner. There, Scalna was truly Scalna, there the truth of our house was encapsulated, inaccessible and imparticipable with respect to all the other houses of the town.

Back when I used to draw with my colored pencils, and then in the days of *The Black Arrow* and *Billy Budd*, the library was only complementary to the yard, where likewise I had my spots for drawing and reading: but later, with the first signs of corruption (maybe it was when the northern wall came crumbling down and the cherry laurel took its place, or perhaps it was as early as the fall of the larch), it became the merciful refuge that excluded everything else. With my grandparents, who encouraged me not to sit in there collecting dust, I invoked exams and the need for a table capable of

158

supporting dictionaries and stacks of paper, although, had I but wanted, I could have managed outside, too, under the blackthorn or the fir tree.

To my changed relationship with that place, the two French windows gave further testimony: once always left open (I remember the sheets of paper moved by the breeze, the forever insufficient paperweights), and in the end always closed, no matter the weather, even if it meant melting from the heat. In terms of the rear window, which framed the garden, a round hillock, and, farther in the distance, the lake broken up by cypresses, I simply closed the panels; but in terms of the other, which opened out onto the narrow balcony running along the front of the house, I closed even the shutters so as not to see the bare sky every time I glanced up, there where my heart held fixed the blackish-green barrier of the fallen larch and cedar.

But there was another reason for keeping everything shut. As I've already mentioned, we had the Baldi family for neighbors. First and foremost, the Baldis were numerous: two grandparents, there as here, but with aunts and uncles too, and their children and sons- and daughters-in-law, and then the grandchildren—five of them!—who were more or less the same age as my sister and I, and who were for the two of us the only real Baldis. Since they had a small house, and weren't homebodies like us, all of them (when none were off taking a swim in the lake) tended to spend the long days gathered in their yard, a yard that was similarly small and therefore incapable of granting a seemly amount of personal space to each family member; and yet it was, evidently, to their constant liking. From there rose up a chorus at once senile and childish: shouting cadenced with bursts of laughter, if not scolding, as well as the bouncing of balls, a nearly uninterrupted chorus from morning till night that reached my ears over our southern wall. If on top of hearing I wished also to see, I merely had to go up to the library on the third floor, and from there look out on the balcony: but this was something I almost never did when I was little because I didn't notice the noise yet, and then, when I was older, because it would only have redoubled my suffering. Thinking about it now, I have to admit that it's strange: that trees, walls, arbors, gritstone sinks, and many other things out there in the town had actually changed, deteriorating little by little or getting crushed by the elements or by the ignorance of man, but in any case changing, while those voices next door, on the contrary, had apparently always been there, and only their echo had changed inside *me*, becoming more and more resounding until I eventually could stand them no longer and would ask my mother irritably, the few times she came to stay with us, "Are you sure? It was like this—really, *just* like this—even when I was little? It's *always* been like this?" And as much as she tried to convince me, and as much as I knew she must have been right, I could not wrap my head around it.

Hence I bolted the library windows shut, and, besides a few insolent peaks, the voices stayed outside. And outside, too, remained the agonizing noises of the town—the motorbikes growing more numerous each year, the honking of arrogant Milanese vacationers, and still more wound-up children and self-satisfied mothers—although at least in this case I knew that the change wasn't only in me: rather, there were new noises out there that hadn't been around before, and the old sounds, the ones I had loved (the shouting of "Fish here . . . *fiiish!*" and of "Knife sharpener: bring out your knives!" and the *bong! bong!* of gas cylinders being unloaded off a truck), had all disappeared.

The production of sounds was therefore something the Baldis had in common with the town's other inhabitants, locals and holidaymakers alike, such that their household was assimilated into the whole. But there was more. Ever since I was little, I had noticed our neighbors' stupefying *connivance* with the town. While my sister and I never went beyond our front gate, except for an occasional errand, and always played in our house or yard without ever commingling with outsiders, the five young Baldis spent a good part of their days out in the street together with other children, or would otherwise pass the time at the oratory or riding their bicycles in gangs of eight, of ten, of twenty, and even when they were in their own yard would never fail to call someone to come in and join big and intricate group games, and, in short, only at nightfall would the various bloodlines separate and could an onlooker finally tell who were the siblings and who were the visitors, and so perceive some slight sense of order in that ramified admixture of legs and Mottarello ice cream bars, of lollipops and rackets.

They had even come looking for us a couple of times, a long time ago. Let's suppose I was in the kitchen cutting out figures from a magazine, or stirring flour in a saucepan to make the glue for my goopy concoctions, when my grandma came in and notified me that the Baldis were at the front gate and wanted to know if we would go with them to the quarry.

"What do you mean, the quarry?"

"To the quarry, on your bicycles. There are other kids too."

"How many are they? A lot?"

"I didn't count. Come on, make up your mind. They're waiting for you two."

"We need to decide right away? *Now*?"

"Yeah, they're all ready to go."

"And Agostina?"

"She says she'll only go if you do."

"Couldn't they go ahead and we'll see about joining them later?"

"Well, that doesn't make sense. If you're going, you should go with them now."

"Agostina can't go on her own?"

"She says she's too embarrassed, that she'll only go with you. But run along, it'll do you good."

"No, no."

"Go tell them then."

"Can't you tell them?"

And she told them, while I spied on the scene from the window. After a few other instances, they stopped coming to look for us.

Both the two of us and the Baldis, for that matter, acted in a manner consistent with the conduct of our respective families: while our grandparents were rather reserved and wary of others—and our mom and dad hardly ever there—their family clan welcomed the life of the town with open arms, munificent in taking the time to chat at the general store, considerate of the initiatives of the parish (punctually hanging floral ornaments on their front gate for St. Anna's Day or generously gambling at every charity raffle), regulars on the bench in the piazza in the evening, and always ready, with sympathetic nods of the head, to inquire into Luigino's progress at school or into Mrs. Carla's cystitis. I noticed this difference constantly, from thousands of clues. In fact, this alone would have sufficed: when I would go to the general store to buy bread and eggs, I had to pay and then wait for change; the Baldis, on the other hand, never paid, and when they were done shopping, Mrs. Lucia would look in the drawer for her greasy blue notebook (scientific series, the kind displaying a drawing of an eyeball in a plastic square aperture) and therein, with complicit understanding, would "make a note of it." In all those years, never in the absence of correct change did I see a note taken on my account: I always had to wait for Lucia to go out and break a bill.

Only attending mass, I realize now, could have bound us somewhat to the ecumene, but the only one of us who went was my grandmother, or occasionally my grandfather. After our earliest summers there, my sister and I were "exempted"—my mother had been quite clear on this point—and so we missed that one opportunity for interaction. Not that I minded. On the contrary, the unnatural silence of Sunday mornings, that suspension of all activities, seemed to grant my games a more piquant flavor, a greater aura of enchantment; but in spite of this, if from the third floor I happened to witness the Baldis leaving for mass (formally dressed, assembled as a single block in their yard as they waited for stragglers in order to head off all together) I managed to feel—for a second, then it passed—a sense of ignorant exclusion. They were only going to be bored to death, I had no doubt about that, and yet, I'd say to myself, who knows, maybe sometimes boredom is less sad than fun.

And so, with the passing of time, I went less and less often onto that balcony. Indeed, what else was there to see, looking to my right, if not eyesores? Just as the voices of the Baldis had year after year become more intolerable to my ear, some of the saliences of their yard and of their house, previously unremarked, had gradually grown more and more perceptible to my eye until they finally colonized my consciousness like flat-out insults: that pretentious English lawn, for example, so unlike our natural yard and so at odds with the idea of the countryside; or those little gneiss walkways, that consistently raked white gravel, those affected flower beds! I looked at our canopy swing underneath the blackthorn tree and saw a solid structure of rather rusted iron, tinted a nice faded green, and so heavy it took four tile slabs underneath to keep it from sinking into the earth; I looked at theirs and saw a modern little thing suited for a city terrace, made of white plastic-sheathed aluminum, its red-fringed cushions streaked with yellow and coffee-colored stripes. I looked at our trees, or thought of the ones that had fallen, and saw serious trees, conifers and persimmon trees, medlar and chestnut trees: I looked over there and saw ridiculous, artistically grouped birches, crape myrtles, shrubs fit for a seaside boardwalk in Nice, apartment plants with shiny fat leaves. And in the midst of it all were pool mattresses and beach umbrellas, bulging sunglasses and bulky portable radios, motorbikes and barbecue grills, and the children of the former children, as if the countryside were not something intimate and serious and profound, an eternally autumnal or wintery place even in the summer, a world through which to walk in cumbersome boots and fustian socks and nasty old rain jackets, struggling to lift one's heavy feet as if owing to an increased gravitational force, a world reeking of earth and barn, of old resinous wood, of rotted leaves and mushrooms: a slow, muffled world, where to be even more alone than one was in the city, but a more beautiful, more yearned-for solitude, among the fireflies and the blackbirds, the spindly spiders and the stag beetles . . . Over there, however, it looked like a beach (why in the world didn't they just go to the seaside then?). And I should have gone out on the balcony to find myself face to face with such a shameless display of summertime, when even at the height of August I did everything to deny the season's existence and to act as though it were fall, when chestnuts are harvested and no one is around? Better to keep everything shut, including the blinds, and should the French window facing the lake not provide sufficient light for study, then switch on the lights, and never come out.

Yes, the town has changed. Even locked away in the library, I sense the changes, I feel them one on top of the other like whiplash scars on my back, the oldest still as scandalously present as the freshest lesions. There was the cyclist's yard, full of tires and chains, with an enormous bathtub overflowing with weeds: they turned it into a parking lot. There were nameless streets, which everyone referred to with names out of local lore, dictated by the heart: they put up street signs, and the "wolf road" became Via Matteotti. The nicest thing of all beyond the town was a big stone washbasin, and anyone waiting for the bus used to sit on its edge in the shade and sink their hands into the freezing water, which seemed clean even when cloudy with soap. Now there's only a bollard dividing the traffic, and when I say on the bus that I'm going "as far as the washbasin," the ticket inspector just looks at me suspiciously. To this fervent spirit of renewal, the Baldis appeared to adhere not only without any resistance, but with their own special enthusiasm. Among the things that struck me most, in their behavior, was undoubtedly their industriousness: a constant hammering, drilling, repainting, a love of substitution for its own sake, a crazed scrambling for what was new, modern, "young." I looked at our house and theirs and found the two ever more divergent, one moored in a near-mineral fixedness (some things had gone, yes, but as atrocious as those losses were, they hadn't altered the house's innermost essence), the other immersed in the flow of time that carried it away, reshaping it in its image, changing its chemistry. One house goes while the other stays, I thought, and I felt dwelling in our home the spirit of death, as if there had been two twins of whom only one had grown up, combining his bodily cells with the elements of the world in a regenerative union, while the other had died a baby and shriveled up just as he was, a little mummy; but then I would revolt against this idea, and I told myself that if the spirit of life corresponded to the chain of devastation being perpetrated beyond that wall, if living meant dying over and over again, well then, death was there too, on the Baldis' side, and uglier there than here.

Musing that there must have been a time when the two houses had not been so distinct from one another, I was frightened by the realization that I carried with me not only my own memories, but also the memories of others: I managed to suffer for them, too, for what they had lost and for what they hadn't missed in the first place; and even when I had never known what came before, I nonetheless perceived its shadow behind the current state of things, like an incensed ghost calling out for revenge. The whole town was populated with these shades; they flitted hither and thither, and I felt as though I were the only one who saw them. And even when I threw a glance into yards I had never seen before, during ever rarer and ever briefer bicycle rides, I could scarcely defend myself from the onslaught of more shadows, and more shadows still, which rose up from all over, asserting their mute afflictions. I'd come back home in a state of distress, weighed down with pleas and entreaties that left me in a daze, and of those restless wraiths I felt myself the keeper, like the last minister of a creed that in him alone survives.

On the side opposite the Baldis, behind the northern wall, the one that would later fall, lived Flora. I never knew her age: I had only ever seen her hunched and covered in wrinkles, wearing the same light-blue headscarf with white polka dots. Her yard was nothing but a big vegetable garden, with green beans, cucumbers, cabbages, zucchinis—and where she didn't grow vegetables, she kept her chickens. The two narrower ends of that yard's perimeter consisted, toward the road, of Flora's cottage—only one floor—and, at the opposite end, of the side of our old hayloft. I would often go up in that hayloft, looking out from a little balcony, to talk to Flora's dog, who responded every time I called him,

167

contentedly standing up on his hind legs. He was called Tabù, and after his death his successor was called Tabù, both small, long-haired dogs covered in gray and black spots. By conversing with Flora, who would always interrupt her gardening to walk over to the bottom of the hayloft—and even when inside would come out at the first bark—I realized that, for her, there was no first and second Tabù: it was a single dog, always one and the same. She would pet him on the head and tell me in the meantime about episodes from years past, when *that* Tabù couldn't have been born yet: "Oh, you remember," she said to him, taking a paw, "that time you ran away and I almost died of fright?" Or: "And what about Bianchina? You sure did like Bianchina, didn't you?" and of this Bianchina character no one in town retained the faintest memory, there was no telling for how many years she had been in the ground. Actually, a few details led me to suspect that certain stories pertained to a third dog, or even a fourth—who knows, maybe there was a succession of Tabùs that stretched all the way back to Flora's childhood, to a mythical Ur-Tabù . . . I myself, who knew the last two dogs, preserve a joint memory of them, and already at the time I felt it wasn't right to try to sever their stories. In fact, I told myself that I, too, after Flora's death, would name my dog Tabù, and I'd look for one just like that: a furry little mutt who was black and gray, prominently whiskered, and with kind yellow eyes.

There were summers throughout which Tabù was my principal companion. When talking to him from the hayloft was no longer enough for me, I'd run over to see him ("Grandma, I'm going over to see Tabù!" I announced on my way out, and, hearing his name, he let out a single "Broo!" as if to say, "It's true!"). Out of the whole town, Flora's house and garden constituted the only area to which it seemed right for me to extend the name of Scalna, as if no wall stood between her and us. I felt good over at her place, cuddling Tabù while he delighted in my presence, and she delighted in the both of us. There wasn't a single book in that house, and yet it was fine just as it was; it wasn't like other houses, which seemed uninhabitable to me without books. There, everything was beautiful, everything weighty with history; I believe that besides the lightbulbs, there wasn't a single object that didn't date back to before the war. When Flora is no longer with us, I thought, this house should be turned into a museum, and defilers beware, lest they touch a thing; then I felt ashamed for thinking this, and I said to myself that it would be wonderful if many identical Floras followed one after the other, each with her own Tabù, so that nothing changed. She would look at me with her hazelnut eyes, squinting a bit due to her poor eyesight, and I felt as though she were reading my thoughts.

My grandparents never said it outright, but I knew they considered the regularity with which I visited that old woman strange, when all I would've had to do upon coming out onto the street was turn to the right instead of the left and ring the doorbell at the first gate in order to find myself in the company of kids my own age. I gathered this from indirect hints ("There's a sound like a ping-pong game coming from the Baldis. Why don't you go over and see?"), but for me there was really no choice. Nevertheless, I realized to my chagrin that there were times when those two worlds met, contaminating each other. It happened whenever Flora, after walking out onto the street to stretch her legs, found the Baldis' welcoming front gate open, as was often the case: she'd then enter naturally, sure to encounter after a few meters one of the old aunts with whom to chat (I'd immediately recognize her voice, and go onto the balcony to check: oh, how out of place she looked on that horrible canopy swing!). But it also happened, and the manner was even more offensive, whenever one of the little Baldis paid her a visit, actually entering her home: "Grandma, I'm going over to see Tabù!" I'd yell, unsuspecting and happy, but then I'd find one of them sitting there—Franco, let's say, or Claudia—and in a flash all my happiness would desert me. "My goodness, so much nice company," Flora would say. "Did you see? Franco's come over." And to Franco, "Did you see? Michele's come over." On those occasions, I'd immediately rush out to the garden to talk to Tabù, and I'd try not to go back inside until the other kid was gone. But sometimes it also transpired that, while I was outside, other little Baldis came to join their brother or sister, smugly parking themselves on all the available chairs: I'd recognize them from their voices without having to see, and I'd stay just as I was, lying low amid the green beans, with the dog curled up at my feet and with my soul under siege. Tabù seemed to understand, for he also stayed hunkered down, hidden; we looked at each other in silence until, moved by his solidarity, which I thought must have cost him no small effort, I rewarded him with his favorite game: "Who wants the drumstick?" I whispered, and moving my fingers as shears, I pretended to cut off his thigh; "And you, ma'am? A piece of the breast?" and back down to carving, "Now that's a tasty-looking morsel, mmmm . . . marbled—who wants it?"

and *chop*, off went another piece; he would fly into ecstasies and lie with his belly in the air to offer me his heart and liver, keeping still in anticipation of the next cut, purring with pleasure like a cat. But eventually I had no choice but to go back, even if the intruders were still present. Tabù stayed where he was, looking disappointed, but I only needed to reassure him as I walked away ("And on tomorrow's menu, Tabù fricassee with a side of green peas!") for his stubby little tail to swing like a pendulum. Passing back through Flora's house, I'd mumble a quick goodbye, directed only at her, then immediately exit. How nice it would have been, I thought whenever one of those regrettable conjunctions occurred, to be able to go directly into Flora's garden from our yard by propping two ladders against the wall! But the most excruciatingly awkward moments came in later summers, when the Baldis and I were about twenty years old and, upon running into one another at Flora's house, had no idea what to say, no idea what to do. Though alike in age and sharing a common language and hometown, living in wall-to-wall proximity every summer, our houses soldered one to the other, we met one another only there, on that neutral ground, as if to sign an armistice among other world powers. Naturally, the Baldis addressed me informally, to which I, ever more embarrassed by that hint of familiarity (oh, all it would have taken was an actual smile on my part for it to have run rampant!) responded with a generic "Hello." Now that Tabù was old and spent his days inside curled up by the woodstove, I no longer had any excuse to run off to the garden—nor could I, in front of those witnesses, say to him, "What do I see? The pope's nose has been left over!" or "Chomp chomp, these spareribs are delish!" Still, while I sat next to him and let the rest of them talk, my fingers drew the virtual lines of those cuts on his fur, dividing him up into segments like the diagram of a cow hanging at a pedagogical butcher's shop: his quivering told me that he needed no narration to recognize the old game. "Ah, Michele has always loved my Tabù," Flora commented; I looked up for a second, gave the blandest of smiles, then focused back on my task.

All of this was already rather dismal, but there was no shortage of even more unpleasant episodes. The time with the lamp, for instance. Next to her bed, Flora had a bluebell-shaped light fixture attached to the wall roughly forty centimeters above her nightstand. This lamp consisted of a brass stem, a ceramic bulb holder, and a corolla of sandblasted glass with a blue meander along its rim. The stem had come unstuck from the plate screwed to the wall—in my recollection, it had always been that way—and stayed in place only by virtue of its inner electrical wire; the corolla was full of cracks after years of knocking and rubbing against the wall; and the string for turning the light on and off was completely frayed. Regardless, *that* was Flora's lamp, and imagining another would have been wholly beyond me. In fact, I remember that once, upon hearing in a university auditorium that for the famous philosopher from Stuttgart "only the real is rational," it was none other than that same lamp which popped into my head, Flora's lamp with its incredibly rational cracks and frayed ends. But one day . . . one day I went over to see Flora and, instead of her lamp, I saw an adjustable spotlight, a lacquered red shade, an opalescent bulb.

"What is that?!"

"Did you see what a nice thing the Baldis did? They noticed that the lamp I had before was giving off sparks, and the next day they came over with this new one."

So, it had happened. So, through their recurrent presence, the Baldis had finally succeeded in ushering a postwar item into that house! An object that belonged to the category of the new and the young, in other words, their category! A signature, a flag planted to mark an outpost, a sort of altimeter: "Lieutenant, what is the situation on Summit 1945?" "The men have reached spotlight altitude, Captain." "Good, maintain that altitude." It reminded me of "Find the Odd One Out" in my puzzle magazine, and looking around I picked at my leisure: 1) enameled iron basin, blue on the outside, white on the inside, chipped; 2) rusted Flit bug spray, varnished tin cylinder, boxwood knob; 3) brass bed warmer, coal-fired, art nouveau perforation, beechwood handle; 4) "Glasnost" model spotlight, designer U. Bottarelli & Associates, LuxDecor, Limbiate.

"But do you like it?"

"I still need to get used to it, but they told me it's nice, that it was the newest one they had . . . "

"There'll be no need to get used to it. You still have the old one, I hope."

Bringing the lamp to Luino, finding a lovingly patient electrician, returning when he had finished the job, disassembling the intruder, and restoring things to their proper order was a weeklong endeavor.

"And what will I say to the Baldis?"

"That you really appreciate the thought they put into it, but now that your lamp doesn't spark anymore, you don't need a new one . . . Besides, aren't you happier this way?"

"Yes."

"Isn't this one nicer? Look at how much nicer it is."

"Yes."

"Then forget about what they say. And to celebrate"—intuitively, that good boy was already wagging his tail—"pieces of Tabù-fish on the grill for all! Swish! Swish! What beautiful steaks of fish—swish!"

I forgot about the spotlight, and almost a month had passed when one evening (the summer was coming to an end, in a few days we'd go back to Milan), my grandmother came up to the library. She almost never went to look for me up there, calling me instead from the yard if she needed me, and so when I saw her standing hesitantly in the doorway, I understood that she had some unwelcome news to share.

"Look, Michele, tell me the truth. Did you go over to Flora's a couple of weeks ago to bad-mouth the Baldis?"

"Me? Why?"

"I bumped into Mrs. Baldi this morning while leaving church, and as we walked back together, we got to talking. First, she asked about you, about your studies, she says that you come across as awfully studious, and then, well . . . she said that her grandkids had their feelings badly hurt because you went to tell Flora that she shouldn't accept gifts from them, that she shouldn't trust them, and things like that . . . Could it be true? I didn't understand, I told her that there must have been a misunderstanding, but she made a strange face, and insisted that her grandkids always tell her the truth . . . "

Smoothing things over took more time than repairing the lamp. First my grandmother got involved, then my poor mother, who after an August spent working had come to join us for the last few days of the month in hopes of being able to relax. The affair lasted until the first day of September, when there were already suitcases strewn about and I finally agreed to meet with the Baldis to clear things up. "Working everything out," my mom instructed me, "means spelling everything out." After which no one spoke of it again. All the same, in the years to come, before going over to Flora's, I would make absolutely sure that the Baldis weren't there, that they were at the lake or at the market, and except for the one time I bumped into Claudia on the street, and in response to her cordial "Hey," I likewise responded with an unprecedented "Hey," our paths never crossed.

It disturbed me, their friendliness. It struck me as a low blow, a clever way of neutralizing my warlike disposition, by now a time-honored legacy I was rightly owed. It wasn't enough that they constantly shouted from morning till night, or that they felt lonely unless they invited over at least ten acquaintances, that they practiced the religion of the spoiled infant and the principle "Kids *have* to yell—they're kids!"; it wasn't enough that every summer they exhibited an additional newborn, perpetually frustrating my hopeful "At least they'll have to get older"; that they offended aesthetic norms with floral Bermuda shorts and yellow tank tops, that they gloried in motorbikes and radios: no, on top of all that, one had to be friendly to them, because they were friendly to us! My grandma never missed an opportunity to remind me of this. "It's unbearable! I'm going over there right now and telling them to go fix that damnable motorbike at the quarry!" I erupted, and in response she recalled to my attention all the favors they'd done us, the phone call to Milan this past winter to notify us that one of our shutters had fallen down, the shopping they did for us at the market in Luino that time when she and my grandfather were under the weather and I wasn't there, the lock on the front gate which Mr. Baldi fixed (oh, I bet he did, with all those tools in whose sounds he so graciously drowns us!), that photocopy they made of the cadastral map, which is so hard to come by . . .

"I'll tell them where they can put their friendliness," I thought as I went back into the library and bolted all its portals shut. "I'd rather have the Butcher of Treblinka for a neighbor, so long as he's quiet, or a Désiré Landru, and sit there watching the black smoke rising slowly from his chimney."

My grandparents' gratitude toward the Baldis, I clearly realized, was stronger than my remonstrations.

"Ah, what an inviting assortment of apricots," I said one day, coming down to the kitchen and reaching for them.

"Don't touch. They're not for us."

"Not for us? But they're from our tree . . . "

"They're for the Baldis."

"For the Baldis?!"

"They're always so nice to us, and have always brought us pears over the years . . . "

"Then you should leave well enough alone, because maybe this will be our lucky year and they'll stop bringing them. If we start up too, we'll be setting off a domino effect of which we'll never see the end. And, anyway, it's not like we asked for those pears. Honestly, I could have gladly done without them."

But no, nothing to be done. Christian altruism, good-neighborliness, middle-class terror of "owing" something, a desire for pears: all of it irresistibly contributed to my defeat. Worthless were my protests, as were my most stubborn forms of dissent ("We don't have any other fruit. Either pears or nothing." "Then nothing, I'd sooner starve to death!" "Don't be silly. Come on, eat this pear." "Never!").

Other times, in my exasperation, I would address the issue in broader terms: I tried to make my grandparents understand that the Baldis and I had nothing in common, and that the simple fact that we were neighbors, separated only by a wall, did not engender in and of itself any kind of affinity or phratry, nor should it make such sentiments of kinship appear obligatory; that interlocutors must be *chosen* and not *inflicted*, that maybe our ideal neighbors were five or a hundred kilometers away (with them, then, by all means, the exchanging of pears and greetings, and visits too, card games and chess matches, deep conversations, even weddings!); that if someone is a jerk they don't cease to be one just because they live near you (au contraire!!!); that, in short, when we came out to the country it wasn't only for the fresh air and the temperate climate, but also to spend some time relaxing in isolation, whereas thanks to them it was as if a piece of Milan always followed us there; that one shouldn't be moved by some measly gift or smile, that there are superior forms of friendliness, such as discretion, above all, and respect for others' peace and quiet—if they started showing a bit more acoustic discretion, then you'd see, oh, you'd see how friendly I could be, and how many apricots I'd bring them, and seasonal fruits of all kinds!

If we were at least equally matched—I'd then think to myself—if there were as many of us and we were just as loud, so as to pay them back holler for holler, uproar for uproar! Instead, we simply had to learn to live with their crushing numeric superiority, because now that the five "kids" had married, the Baldis showed up every July with a new rug rat in tow. Hence a geometric progression, hence in twenty years they would have doubled, hence over there the future held indescribable crowds, while over here—emptiness, and just a few decrepit old-timers wandering through vast spaces . . . Yes, just a few old-timers, because both my sister and I knew, without ever talking about it, that we would never have children and at most we'd perhaps bring our respective consorts along, just the right number of people for a melancholic game of scopa: cards, golds, and prime, twenty-one, oh, you two were lucky tonight, but tomorrow we'll make a comeback, right, Ludmilla? of course, Michele, we're going out to look at the moon, are you two coming? no, thank you, it's already ten o'clock and I have to put the kettle on for the hot-water bottle, yes, actually it is rather late, it's a bit cold too, shall we go upstairs? let's go upstairs, goodnight, Agostina, goodnight, Edgardo, goodnight, Ludmilla, goodnight, Michele. Or worse, worse: not even married, but just the two of us, embittered and querulous, forced by our ineptitude to rely on the services of insolent country gardeners and avaricious craftsmen, exposed to the affronts of the uncaught thief and to the vulgarities of local lovers who, hopping the gate, would come at night to do their dirty business in our yard ("You sure it's safe? What if they see us?" "Who do you think'll see, those two geezers who go to bed before the sun even goes down?"), and at the foot of yon spruce you'll find condoms and cans in the morning, and wishing them death does not placate you, rather may they choke on globs of their own blood and may they suffer the scorpion's bite! Or no, worse still, forced by poverty to cede a part of the house or the yard to the Baldis, we'd consequently be confined to a few cramped rooms from which to witness the ruination: trees chopped down to make way for silly gazebos, a mansard added to the hayloft by some ostentatious architects, blithesome benches made from logs that scream to the world of their lost majesty, and gneiss everywhere, and flower bed enclosures . . . And if my sister should abandon me too? If a late-in-life leman whisked her away, to a little apartment in Celle or Rapallo? If she died before me? Yes, I could already picture myself clearly, barricaded in my library like a usurer among shelffuls of pledges, with a forever unmade sofa bed covered in crumbs, and a Primus hot plate encrusted with curdled milk, and heaps of dirty clothes on the floor: a sordid old man obliged to ask for permission before going outside to use his filthy outhouse, and who like a local boogeyman becomes the threatened punishment for children!

When I then thought of Flora, how different her condition seemed to me! Alone, yes, and in a little cubbyhole, but sure of what was hers, and serene as a placid Baucis, with only ourselves for neighbors, the *ante quem* of her antique objects, and the company of her immortal Tabù . . . The mere idea of Tabù was irresistible: immediately I had to abandon books and notepads and run over to him, and then, after stepping foot in Flora's home, pretend at first not to have seen him there, curled up by the woodstove: "Good day, ma'am, they told me that you have some fine round steaks here, but my golly, where are they? I don't see them, wherever might they be, but zounds zounds I smell rounds, oh, there we are, just what I'm after, so let's see, a few slices for the veal with tuna sauce, chop! chop! chop! and the rest diced (slice 'n' dice, as they say!) . . . But what do I see? This isn't a round, it's an Andean faun. We'll have to debone it . . . "

Nowadays, when melancholy overtakes me, it is impossible for me to carve, to conduct the loving incision. It came to pass a few years ago: we had just arrived at Scalna, only time enough to carry up the suitcases to our rooms and to air out the library, to check quickly that the damp hadn't marred any of the books, and then off I went! Down the stairs, flying across the uncut lawn to the hayloft, and up that flight of stairs, jumping over the whetstones and blades scattered on the steps, until I finally looked out.

I remember that it wasn't the absence of chickens, nor the omnipresence of weeds, that told me that the last—the gravest—devastation of Scalna had been wrought: it was, rather, the green bean trellis, widowed and naked, which spoke to me of a state of abandonment that must have stretched back many months, back through the whole spring at least, and maybe earlier, maybe to the fall, shortly after our last departure for Milan. I ran into the street but Flora's front gate was locked, I looked around, but there was no one to ask, I went back inside, "Grandma, Grandma, Flora's not there! She's gone!" I rushed up to the library and from there onto the balcony, everything shut over at the Baldis' too, oh, how many times, at the outset of summer, had those closed shutters filled me with joy, portending a few days of unforeseen silences, if not indeed intoxicating me with the monstrous hope that, yes, maybe this was my lucky year, maybe on account of some miraculous chain of events none of them would be able to come for the entire summer (the next day, all it took was the first squeal, the first comradely "whoopee!" to send me crashing into the gloomiest of moods): now, instead, I cursed those shutters and that delayed arrival, for they could have explained, recounted, since they always knew everything, enmeshed as they were in local life.

Two days of anguish passed, during which I dared not ask anyone anything. I could have asked Lucia, but how to even approach her (and there in the store, in front of all those gossipy little women!) when for over twenty years, in order to deter her clinging loquacity, I had consistently stuck to the curtest indications: "Eight rolls of bread and a liter of milk, whole." "Is that loaf all that's left? I'll take it." I didn't know anyone else in town—the cyclist had moved to Germignaga the year before, unable to bear the pain of seeing parked cars where he had once delighted himself with pedal cranks and chains (how I'd hated him for surrendering that yard, wishing him precisely that heartbreak), the trattoria was long gone by now, the blacksmith was dead, and so much time had passed since I'd last seen the cobbler that I wondered if he had ever existed in the first place . . . No, it was just as well to wait for the Baldis, sooner or later they always arrived, they would be able to explain. In any other circumstances it would have irked me enormously to rely on them, but now things were different, now Flora was involved, as was Tabù. Who knew where he was, that dear little mutt, that dearest prime cut!

They arrived Saturday afternoon, and this struck me as purposely done in order to allow my grandmother to inquire the very next day, when leaving church. And so I instructed her to that end, pedantically repeating over and over the points necessitating elucidation (especially in regards to Tabù who, insofar as he was a canine, would no doubt rouse to a lesser degree her Christian compassion).

I was on the balcony, that Sunday morning, when the whole tribe assembled in the garden for its ecclesial expedition. Keeping out of sight behind an arch, I counted them: there were eighteen, meaning the rule had been respected and that year, too, another newborn had arrived to increase their already solid ranks . . . I tried to glean something from their expressions, to anticipate what they would tell my grandmother, but was this anything more than vain speculation? As if—no matter what had befallen Flora, even the most horrible, the most sorrowful of fates—too many months had not already passed for any sign of it to still remain in people like them, people who were entirely imbued with the spirit of life and of renewal, and, for that very reason, were given not only to forgetting in a hurry with eyes facing forever ahead, but also to lightening deaths and tragedies of all that is definitive and absolute in them, incorporating losses in a forward-looking vision of replacement and compensation, and of consolatory statutes: yes, the kind of people who, while promulgating that "life goes on," do not sense that life will no longer be as before, because in it death, too, goes on, augmenting all the while, and that no offspring will be able to fill the void left by your papa, not even if you've scrambled to bring into the world one hundred fifty rug rats who replicate his irises and nose, his jawline and his name. And reflecting on these things, while they had all left and only the lastborn and an aunt remained in the yard, I realized something curious: that yes, they were extremely informed about everything, but on the condition that it lived, for of things and persons passed I alone was keeper, I alone preserved orderly memory; as if the work in an archive had been divvied up between us, to them the modern part, to me the old, one folder to you and another to me, a stack of files over there and another over here . . . And I, I hoped to wrest from them some emotion with which they might pay their respects to the past, a backward-looking sentiment, something that went beyond the naked facts?

Finally, my grandmother came back. Running to meet her on the walkway, I considered for the first time how untoward it had been of me to compel her to question the Baldis when for years I had been unforgiving whenever I found her indulging them, no matter how slightly. But now what mattered most was finding out, and I found out.

Flora was very sick, and in need of constant care; over the course of the past winter, the arthritis and diabetes that had afflicted her for so many years (what, the Baldis had replied with amazement, we didn't know?) had worsened until she could no longer walk on her own, and in the end she spent her days in bed, with some women from the town taking turns assisting her; a nurse came every day from Laveno for her medicine and shots, but things couldn't go on in that manner: Flora didn't have anything put away, she lived off her social pension, and we knew like everyone else how expensive medicine was (but no! I didn't know, and only then did I also realize that I didn't know and had never wondered how Flora got by, how she had lived up to that point in time) . . . And so she had sold the house and the land to a nurseryman from Brezzo di Bedero, and had checked herself into a nursing home in Cittiglio, where she was currently staying, and where they, the Baldis, had gone to see her for Easter. She didn't mind it all that much there, she said, but she hadn't given up hope on being able to return to her home, which by a precise contractual agreement the new owner had committed to keeping vacant and unchanged in order to rent it out to her, should she ever request it, until the day she died.

And Tabù? They hadn't talked about him. Hadn't talked about him? Why not? Oh, my Tabù, excluded from human commiseration! I ran into the street like a madman, the Baldis' front gate was ajar, I flung it wide open without slowing down my sprint and burst right into their yard: for the first time, after all those years, I found myself on the other side. Fortunately, all the Baldis had gone into the house to change out of their church clothes into Bermudas and bathing suits: only the old lady, not far from the entrance, was still outside, digging in a flower bed.

"Ma'am, please!" I said, before she could even look surprised. "I know you spoke with my grandma, but you didn't mention him . . . You see, we'd like . . . I'd like to know about Tabù, what happened to him, if you've heard any news?"

"Tabù?"

"Yes, Flora's dog."

"Like the brand of licorice?"

"Yes, yes—your grandchildren never talked to you about him?"

"Oh, I knew she had a dog, but I don't know what happened to it. I think she gave it to someone in town to look after, but I couldn't tell you who, maybe you could ask the parish priest. When we went to see her, she didn't talk about a dog. Oh, and isn't she a poor woman too . . ."

"She didn't talk about him because you didn't ask!" I thought, as I hurried to the church. And, then, why "too"? Why lump her in with the unspecified suffering of the world, with some commonly shared affliction? Weren't we speaking only of her, of Flora who was suffering from a particular sorrow that was hers and hers alone, and which one could neither lighten by partaking in it, nor complicate through the addition of other painful qualities? I didn't really understand, but there was something in that "too" that I didn't like, something congregational.

I found the priest folding his vestments at the back of the now deserted church. He eyed me suspiciously, flaunting a level of surprise that seemed intended only to inspire guilt for my total absence at mass. He didn't know that, as a little child, I had gone to that church even before him, when Scalna had a different priest, a big, burly guy with a large black beard, who during the sermon would hammer his heavy fists on the altar, and who due to a cannula in his throat spoke with a gurgling, monstrous voice that fascinated me. As a matter of fact, if that priest had stuck around, I could have still gone to church every now and then; but instead, for his combative heterodoxy, they had relocated him to some little out-of-the-way church way up in Valcuvia, while sending a different priest to Scalna every three or four years, each with the same civil face, each far from that first model of priest, the only one I considered to be legitimate, cannula and all.

I had to introduce myself by describing my grandmother, even though I immediately realized that the association with such a fine familial example of religious observation only managed, by means of contrast, to make him judge me more harshly. Then I mentioned Flora: "Which Flora?" he asked. "There must be at least four in town—four Floras."

"I mean Flora, *the* Flora, the one yea high and yea wide who lived in such and such a house, and who's now in Cittiglio."

"Ah, Flora Collini."

For the first time in my life, I heard Flora's last name, and it made a strange impression on me. To that too—as to the state of her finances, the tenor of her life, and her general health—I had never given a thought. Whose daughter was Flora? Did she still have relatives? And how old could she be? I realized that I not only didn't know the answers, but had never even asked myself the questions. And her past? I knew that she had always done rural work, that she had owned a little farmhouse up in Pira, with a cow and a goat, and that when we were little my sister and I had once gone up there with her . . . But the rest? Was she a widow, or had she never been married? And was she born and raised in Scalna, or had she moved there from another village? Had she always lived in that little house? And . . . oh my, how many questions! For whatever reason, they only came to me when speaking with others, as if I had no choice but to assume their point of view . . . Perhaps one cannot love another while remaining completely ignorant of that person's life? I was sure I loved Flora more than anyone else did, even if for me her house was still Hansel and Gretel's cottage, even if I immediately wanted to forget that last name, so that Flora could go back to being just Flora . . .

Tabù: the only question I'd now allow concerned him, a question to which the priest, however, was scarcely able to reply. As far as he could remember, a dog had indeed been given to someone Flora knew, but who wasn't from Scalna, a woman from out of town, maybe a distant cousin of hers, he wasn't sure, a woman who apparently lived in Valganna . . .

No, if I wanted to find that furry little animal, I needed to find Flora and hear directly from her. The summer had just begun, I had all that time ahead of me to go to Cittiglio—I'd go there a little later in the season, when I was ready. Days passed, the first week; then more days and more weeks. From the library balcony I looked toward the north, where I knew Flora's garden lay, hidden behind the cherry laurel hedges (I was no longer brave enough to go up in the hay-loft), and I made a vow for the following day. "Tomorrow I'm going," I would say, and I never went. I wanted to see her, let her know that I hadn't forgotten about her, and there were moments in which my total ignorance regarding Tabù's fate was intolerable for me: but over everything else prevailed my dread, a dread that allowed me to foresee, with astonishing precision, the unforgettable heartache my visit would cause. I was afraid I would find a different Flora, and that I would then have to remember her that way for the rest of my life, as if what awaited me in Cittiglio could in a second drive out hundreds of sweet memories, overshadowing them forever.

I didn't fear so much changes in her person—already considering her ageless—as the discovery that outside of her home, cut out from that backdrop, Flora would no longer be Flora. They'll have taken away her headscarf, I thought, and she'll be all bald underneath, and she won't have her barbarian rings on her hands, and she'll no longer wrap herself in her big violet quilt, and everything around her will be modern, and there will be so much light silhouetting her against the whiteness of the bed that she'll look even more alone, even more lost and out of place. These images led me to loathe myself for my cowardice and my selfishness (and yet, did I not need to safeguard them, those precious memories? Was I not their keeper?); then I'd defer all decisions to the following day. August, too, passed in this way, until it was the last Sunday of the month, and my grandmother, returning from mass, told me that the previous week the Baldis had gone to Cittiglio to see Flora, that they had found her in good spirits, very weak but not in pain, that she had been moved to another room that she shared with an old sick woman with a constant cough but who at least kept her company, that she still never stopped thinking about her home, to which she hoped to return as soon as the doctors gave her permission, and that they could tell she was pleased at their visit. "'Ah, I almost forgot,' Mrs. Baldi then added, 'she also asked about your grandson.'" "About me?" "Yes, she said to send you a big hello from her."

I won't wait until next year, I kept repeating the following day on a Milan street, I'll take advantage of the chestnut harvest in October and come see you, or when people go for the persimmons—actually, maybe I'll make a special trip,

straight from Milan, yes, maybe it will be nicer that way . . .
But October was devoted to a conference and December
was spent proofreading, and so I never budged from the
city. Who could say, maybe if I let the spring pass too, when
I arrived in Scalna for the summer, a great surprise would be
waiting for me, and I would find her at home, perhaps in her
armchair, with a nice furry turkey to carve into lots of piping
hot slices! Yes, she'd come back, I felt that it *had* to happen,
it was predestined in the grand scheme of things. She would
come back, if not that summer then the one after. I would
wait for her, I'd bring her a big bouquet of flowers, and we'd
pick everything up again where we had left off. That summer
passed too, and then the next. I went to Scalna less and less
often, due in part to work, which I couldn't always bring along
with me, but mostly to all the changes that depressed me. As
soon as I arrived from Milan, all it took was a glance at a new
example of corruption or absence for a gloominess to take
hold of me and not loosen its grip until the moment I left.
And so I'd leave earlier than planned, inventing commitments, promising to swing right back up as soon as I could,
and then I wouldn't show my face again. There were times
when, had it not been for my grandparents, I would have fled
back to Milan the very evening of my arrival, such was the
anguish that assailed me as I carried up my suitcase to my
bedroom and, step after step, tried to convince myself that it
was still the same house, don't you see, everything here is as
it was before—what's the problem?—it's still the same house,
always and forever, still yours . . .

And so I hid away more and more in the library, so as to
reduce to a minimum my own vitality and to dull my senses,

not seeing, neither hearing nor touching, not looking up in painful directions, endeavoring to think as little as possible while brutalizing myself with exhausting philological studies or watching a stage of the Giro d'Italia on TV, again more philology in the evening, then a lousy film, now no longer reading as I did before, reading hurt, it sharpened my sensitivity to time and things, and there wasn't a page that didn't bring me back to myself, forcing me to see my existence with the eyes of others (a gruesome dynamic) or to feel my own circumstances resonate anew.

I thought often of Flora, Cittiglio was so close after all, but I would immediately confound the thought, pushing it back down and telling myself that soon she would return, and then, oh, how nice it would be to see her again there, how much greater the surprise and purer the emotion! Like when one is thirsty while walking but in order to enhance the pleasure of that final refreshment scorns any fountains along the way . . . And I felt, too, that in comparison to that assuredness, going to Cittiglio would have amounted to giving up, as if only the fact that I was patiently waiting for her could call Flora back; as if it were, essentially, a test in which the slightest wavering would be enough to compromise ultimate success . . . She herself, upon seeing me walk into that bright room, after an initial smile would have grown sullen. "So it's true," she would have thought, "if he's come too, it means I'll never return, it means I'm already dead." Worse, Flora, worse, it is *I* who have killed you by coming, forgive me, I couldn't hold out, just like when as a child I had to keep my eyes closed while going down the whole dark hallway, another meter and I would be free forever, but I'd open them too early, and all around me I'd see the monsters grinning . . . The very wildness of her garden, for that matter, was the best guarantee that the earth itself was waiting: no new crop, no extraneous, profaning hands, no gardeners subjugated to the bad taste of the wealthy, only the patience of the hardened clods of earth, of the naked loyal trellis; the nurseryman had his hands tied, he, too, had to wait, for Flora (attagirl!) had cornered him with a very precise clause, which she never would have demanded if she wasn't sure of herself, sure that she would come back to turn over the earth and re-dress her trellis.

I was walking by myself along the stream. That afternoon I had finished a little critical contribution, and so I considered myself authorized to take a walk without feeling too guilty. I walked, following the torrent down amid the nauseating summer lilacs and the elder trees; on the rippling surface, water beetles sped by. Coming out at the quarry, I saw that someone was moving under the enormous rusty conveyor belt, the red splotch of a shirt. I took a few more steps, then stopped behind the crane. The person moved again: it was Claudia Baldi. I was unsure whether to turn back into the bramble bush or to walk in her direction, until she saw me too and started to approach. I felt a hot sensation on my face and something heavy on my chest.

How many hours have passed? Two, three, maybe four. Claudia left a while ago, when it was still light out. Now the stars are in the sky and it's beginning to get cold.

*

"But when, when?"

"Three years ago."

"That long? Three years! But it can't be! How, how could I not know?"

"Still, it'll be three years in December."

"But that means she wasn't there long . . . "

"Do you know how many years she was there?"

"Uh, I don't know exactly, not more than two or three . . . "

"Eight."

The wind has picked up and now it's truly cold, but I can't move—not yet. Who knows what my grandparents will think.

"We wondered why in the world you didn't come. We thought you couldn't make it."

"Were there . . . a lot of people?"

"Oh yeah, we were all there, we came in five cars, except Tommasino, who was only a few months old, and Maria Frine, who wasn't born yet. Plus there was the whole town, just think, even the cyclist came, and tons of other people who no one had ever seen in Scalna before. It was a beautiful funeral."

If I listen closely, I can hear in the sound of the water other sounds passing more quickly, a rustling of reeds, little splashes, the chirp-chirp of a lonely cricket. The important thing is not to turn back around, to stay sitting on this pebbly bed, waiting.

"No, he wasn't there—and how could he have been? He must have died who knows how long before, poor mutt,

192

as old as he was. No one ever managed to find out exactly how old . . . "

Soon it will be dawn, but this is the hour. Now it seems that even the water has become still. All I need to do is not turn around, to stay like this a little while longer, petting this nice flat stone reflecting the moonlight. At the first rustling behind my back, I'll know that they have arrived.

Letting It Bleed

A TRANSLATOR'S AFTERWORD

Children's books, comics, puzzles, toy cars, soccer balls, illustrations, the lyrics of songs and lullabies: taken together, the stories in Michele Mari's *You, Bleeding Childhood* represent a cataloguing of objects and texts, a crystallization—through the most personal artefacts—of a childhood, and with it, a life. A literary project such as this could no doubt be deemed obsessive, but for Michele Mari, the highest form of literature is, as he put it in one interview, the kind "that surrenders to its own obsessions." When asked what his own defining obsession was, beyond literature itself, he indicated the following: "That of living life as a continuous mourning for my childhood, for which I have a nostalgic, neurotic fixation. Not because it was a golden age—quite the opposite . . . But because it was the most meaningful thing I ever lived through." Childhood, with all the terrible consequence of its joys and its pain, is revealed in the pages of Mari's stories as an open wound, one that inevitably bleeds into and tinges the years and decades to come, so as almost to blot them out entirely.

Surprising as it may be for anglophone readers who are new to his work, Michele Mari—once a literary outlier in his native Italy thanks to his bookish phantoms and infatuations—is today seen by many Italians as a kind of living legend. His books, from the late 1980s onward, have prefigured disparate trends in literary fiction, from a general revival of the gothic and the fantastic, to the split selves that have come to characterize autofiction. And yet if Mari can now be recognized as an unlikely trendsetter at home, his work is less frequently considered in relation to his actual contemporaries as it is to distant models such as Poe and Melville, or Céline and Gadda. Mari's writing, with its tendency to mimic older authorial voices and styles, in many ways invites such a reading, employing what he himself calls a "literary vampirism" to explore what would be too crude, commonplace, or heartbreaking to talk about otherwise: a method that elevates these topics and, at the same time, renders them more bearable, if not hilarious. In other words, style enables a "process of redemption," of regaining the upper hand on life.

This correlation between literature and real life, however, is not always straightforward. Before producing more overtly autobiographical work, Mari published, beginning with *Di bestia in bestia* (From Beast to Beast) in 1989, three novels that were seemingly of the most fantastical and hyper-literary order: a gothic castle where a man keeps hidden from the world his immense library and his own monstrous twin; a diary from the 1800s investigating the possibility that the young poet Giacomo Leopardi might be a werewolf; a Spanish galleon visited nightly by magical fish whose secret knowledge is coveted not only by a bedridden captain, but also by his Iago-like first mate. A clear theme tying these novels together, in addition to their reproduction of older, largely eighteenth- and nineteenth-century language and literary modes, is that of the double, of one's own freakish or regressive other half. Although the theme might be less apparent in the book as a whole, perhaps it is only with his 1997 collection *You, Bleeding Childhood* that we finally discover a key motivating factor behind Mari's recurring focus on the hidden other. From the first story, in fact, the reader is presented with a Jekyll and Hyde scenario, in which an outwardly respectable—indeed, an outwardly *grown up*—professor decides he must hide away in order to give vent to his truest passions and reread his childhood comics. (Fittingly, the child inside the author who reawakens and relives in his books often isn't Michele Mari at all, but "Michelino," with due diminutive suffix.)

While his use of literary pastiche has led Mari to be read in dialogue with venerated authors of the past—that is, with the "canon"—nowhere is the vast and unconventional nature of his own personal canon more evident than in this collection. By drawing most explicitly on the genres that made him first fall in love with reading in his youth, Mari engages in a process of reevaluation, expansion, and inclusion, subverting common conceptions of what counts as classic literature. Throughout *You, Bleeding Childhood*, a refined and even archaic vocabulary melds fluidly with the lexicons, tropes, and traditions of numerous popular genres, plumbing the emotions a young reader might experience when first encountering infatuating and hair-raising works of horror or adventure, fantasy or sci-fi, not to mention folktales and myths, mysteries, westerns, nautical novels, and so on. This ennoblement of what is often viewed as second- or third-tier literature is carried out continuously, from "The Covers of Urania," an essayistic ode of love and terror to a sci-fi series that introduced the author to "the dark side of literature" simply through the outer appearance of the volumes; to "Eight Writers," in which a supergroup of maritime writers must be disbanded in order to reveal which of the eight is ultimately the greatest, as they battle for supremacy in a heightened fan-fiction of the mind; or again, in the opening lines of "Comic Strips," where a literature professor comes to realize that his childhood comics, still contained in his extensive and invaluable library, hold an "eminence before which all the other books—the 'real' books, the 'serious' books—had to bow down." Such a statement shouldn't be read as simply farcical or provocative: before enrolling in university and setting out to become a professor of Italian literature, Mari himself focused on drawing comics and graphic novellas, even garnering the praise of Italo Calvino. After receiving the sixteen-year-old artist's adaptation of *The Cloven Viscount*—another bloody tale of a split individual—Calvino wrote to him, "I had great fun looking at your *Viscount* comic. Your way of narrating through images is full of witty and effective visual devices ... I'm delighted by your work."

Across Michele Mari's oeuvre, these decisive books from his youth come together with other childhood relics—the comforting and the haunting alike—to form a personal mythology. More than just symbolic items, they are fetishes, in the original sense of the word; or to cite the protagonist of another one of Mari's novels, Walter Benjamin, they have an "aura." At the same time, these artefacts gradually reveal themselves, too, as prisms through which to view others; as talismans that house the essence not only of the author and his past, but also of his most formative relationships: grandparents, neighbors, classmates, and most importantly—and most frighteningly—parents. Of his parents, Mari would write at greater length in his partly fictionalized "horror autobiography" *Leggenda privata* (Private Legend), but the importance of these blood ties is first captured in his stories.

Mari's father was renowned industrial designer Enzo Mari, a domineering figure in reference to whom the author would write that his own "admiration was such as to prevent any healthy antagonism at its inception." Already in a few chance anecdotes in the stories "The Covers of Urania" and "Down There," this father betrays a clear taste for frightening his young son, recounting the unthinkable in a straight-faced manner that appears both scarring and, paradoxically, generous, as though imparting one of the greatest gifts for the development of the author-to-be (an author who is always dead serious even when deadly funny). In "The Man Who Shot Liberty Valance"—one of Mari's most Kafkaesque stories, insofar as it recalls the father–son dialogue and the terrible revelations presented in stories such as "The Judgment"—an imagined conversation between the two men acts as a near manifesto on the emotional power of personal objects. With the central figure of Enzo in this story, one can't help but wonder how much his methodology as a designer and artist, who used household objects such as furniture, calendars, and even toys to convey radical ideas and political values, influenced his son's tendency to see the items that filled the day-to-day of his formative years as more than merely material.

A less apparent but equally impactful presence is the author's mother, the children's book illustrator Iela Mari (née Gabriela Ferrario), who sets the tone and the subject matter of two stories in particular: "War Songs," dedicated to the bloody and sorrowful mountain hymns of the Italian Alpini from World War I, which she would sing as lullabies; and "Jigsawed Greens," in which the puzzles obsessively assembled by mother and son become, in a dizzying, Borgesian escalation, a vector for contemplating the infinite through the infinitesimal. Though all but silent on the page, Iela is everywhere in these stories: in the references to mountains, for one, which are first used as a metaphor in "Jigsawed Greens," before appearing in the songs of those Alpine troops. Iela had been a skilled mountain climber, an activity that became so detached from her married life that Enzo apparently didn't even know about her passion, let alone that she had regularly climbed with the likes of Dino Buzzati, an author who originally made a name for himself with the novella *Barnabo of the Mountains*. As Mari reveals in *Leggenda privata*, such stories seemed to pertain to a different Iela from before, with the pieces of his mother's life appearing impossible to fit together: a mother characterized, in other words, by fragmentation, who already in *You, Bleeding Childhood* imparts a vision of the world broken into puzzle pieces, singing of a military captain who commands that he himself be "into five pieces cut."

In contrast to the frantic anxieties that fill Mari's paternal tales, in these two stories the narrator's profound emotion and nostalgia are perceptible under an analytical veneer, an apparent coldness, as if to mirror a figure who is referred to elsewhere in the collection as the "Fake Mother," one who, even when smiling, dons the emotionless mask of a body snatcher. While Mari evidently feared as a child that his real mother had been replaced by the hollow exterior of an extraterrestrial or pod person, in *Leggenda privata* he also points to the overpowering character of his father as having had a hand in turning her into what can only be described as a shell of her former self, writing "my mother was destined to be colonized, if not by a pod than by him, he who occupied people like a tenant occupies an apartment, renovating it according to the most rational laws."

This father's ability to occupy the minds and colonize the lives of others is felt most intensely in *You, Bleeding Childhood* in "The Black Arrow." When the unnamed Enzo Mari gives Michelino the very same book he has just read—Stevenson's *The Black Arrow*—but in a different translation, the need to live up to his father's expectations, and to enjoy the extraordinary gift as though it were something completely new, leads to a comparative textual analysis and, indirectly, to the birth of the literary scholar and philologist. Here the heightened, grandiloquent style of the narrative voice alludes not only to the tone of Stevenson's novel of medieval knights, but also to the young boy's noble endeavor to rise to the challenge his father has unwittingly presented him with, swelling in an outpouring of words for a relationship seemingly doomed to "mute misunderstanding." It would be hard to imagine a more inspired celebration of the art of translation in the short story form, one that ultimately deems every translation a unique and original work unto itself; and it's worth noting that Mari has turned increasingly to this art form over the last decade, supplying new Italian translations of classics in the genres of adventure (Stevenson's *Treasure Island* and London's *The Call of the Wild*), science fiction (Wells's *The Time Machine*), and horror (naturally, Stevenson's *Strange Case of Dr. Jekyll and Mr. Hyde*), among others.

Translating "The Black Arrow," which includes a painstaking deconstruction of the first line in two Italian translations of a book originally written in English, only enhances Mari's exaltation of translation as an art of immeasurable possibilities and implications. In the English translation of the story, the two incipits analyzed by Michelino are two distinct yet parallel sentences that both differ from Stevenson's original, such that they function simultaneously as translations from English for the story's protagonist and as translations into English for the anglophone reader. Due to this added textual layer, the actual first line of Stevenson's book has been inserted into the English version of the story, though only at the very end; in this way, Stevenson's sentence is revealed as a final counterpart to the two "translated" sentences introduced at the story's outset, and the metaliterary game comes full circle. This isn't the only instance in which, through a process of collaboration with Michele Mari, subtle structural changes have been made to keep elements of anglophone literature legible and coherent when translated *back* into English. In "The Covers of Urania," the titles of the cited books—the majority of which were written by American and English authors—reflect, by necessity, the titles Michelino saw on the Italian covers in question; as a result, the section on "Title translations" that appears in the story has doubled in length in order to function as a more comprehensive key containing the original English titles. Meanwhile, in "Eight

Writers," literary references both explicit and hidden have found their way back into English, with quoted and paraphrased sections of Cesare Pavese's iconic Italian translation of *Moby-Dick*, for one, being replaced by Melville's original, and the more contemporary sounding voice of Mari's "Pavesian" Ahab substituted with the archaic pronouns and conjugations that distinguish the character for anglophone readers.

Finally, this English edition of *You, Bleeding Childhood* includes two beloved stories taken from Mari's first collection, published in 1993, *Euridice aveva un cane* (Eurydice Had a Dog)—two stories that complement the recurring themes and obsessions of his 1997 collection: the accumulation and literal fetishization of objects, a preoccupation with the passing of time, and the impossibility of preserving the past. Replete with dark humor reminiscent of Edward Gorey illustrations, these stories constitute two of the finest examples of Mari's entertaining use of a high gothic mode to write about childhood. And in the story "Eurydice Had a Dog," specifically, Mari's antiquated style matches a young protagonist marked by a morbid antipathy toward other adolescents his age, who gleefully embrace all that is new and contemporary, a dynamic repeated in "And I Am Thy Daemon," "They Shot Me and I'm Dead," and elsewhere.

The first story for which Mari explicitly used his own life as his subject matter, "Eurydice" also familiarizes readers with the much-mythologized house near Lake Maggiore where he spent his summers growing up, in a town first referred to as Scalna and in later works called by its real name, Nasca. "Scalna was never a town," the story opens, and it seems that this line has been something of a self-fulfilling prophecy, with the house and its surroundings shifting over the years to mirror the inner life of the author. Scalna—that is, Nasca—is, today, not a real place but a ghost town, a hardly locatable hamlet where, although everything has closed, everything has kept still, with outward appearances remaining unchanged: on the walls along its main street, the painted words for the tailor or the trattoria are still legible over the doorways. This place has stayed deeply tied to Mari's autobiographical or autofictional work, becoming the setting of "The Black Arrow" and other moments in *You, Bleeding Childhood*, and returning in two of his most personal and horror-inflected novels, *Verdigris* (forthcoming from And Other Stories) and *Leggenda privata*. Though he has split the majority of his adult life between his hometown of Milan and Rome, Nasca is nonetheless where Mari has done most of his writing, in that same library in which he all but entombed himself in his youth, and where he fatally chose that translation of Stevenson. If Mari wrote in "Eurydice Had a Dog" that he fantasized as a child of keeping everything exactly the same in his neighbor's house so as to turn it into a museum, that is largely what he has done with his own home. Through the rusted front gate and down the walkway, up the flights of creaky stairs: there, in the bedrooms, one can still find stacks of puzzle boxes and piles of old toys on the antique furniture; or, resting on the nightstand, a single Urania paperback, perhaps left there from the small hours of the night before, or from decades earlier.

BRIAN ROBERT MOORE
Florence, October 2022

Dear readers,

As well as relying on bookshop sales, And Other Stories relies on subscriptions from people like you for many of our books, whose stories other publishers often consider too risky to take on.

Our subscribers don't just make the books physically happen. They also help us approach booksellers, because we can demonstrate that our books already have readers and fans. And they give us the security to publish in line with our values, which are collaborative, imaginative and 'shamelessly literary'.

All of our subscribers:

- receive a first-edition copy of each of the books they subscribe to
- are thanked by name at the end of our subscriber-supported books
- receive little extras from us by way of thank you, for example: postcards created by our authors

BECOME A SUBSCRIBER,
OR GIVE A SUBSCRIPTION TO A FRIEND

Visit andotherstories.org/subscriptions to help make our books happen. You can subscribe to books we're in the process of making. To purchase books we have already published, we urge you to support your local or favourite bookshop and order directly from them – the often unsung heroes of publishing.

OTHER WAYS TO GET INVOLVED

If you'd like to know about upcoming events and reading groups (our foreign-language reading groups help us choose books to publish, for example) you can:

- join our mailing list at: andotherstories.org
- follow us on Twitter: @andothertweets
- join us on Facebook: facebook.com/AndOtherStoriesBooks
- admire our books on Instagram: @andotherpics
- follow our blog: andotherstories.org/ampersand

CURRENT & UPCOMING BOOKS

MICHELE MARI is one of Italy's most renowned contemporary writers. He has published ten novels, in addition to several short story and poetry collections, and has received prestigious awards including the Bagutta Prize, the Mondello Prize, and the Selezione Campiello Prize. A former professor of Italian literature at the University of Milan, he has translated classic novels by Herman Melville, George Orwell, John Steinbeck, and H. G. Wells. In a survey published by the magazine *Orlando Esplorazioni* in 2015, Mari was ranked the contemporary Italian author most likely to be read by generations to come.

BRIAN ROBERT MOORE has translated *A Silence Shared* by Lalla Romano, *Meeting in Positano* by Goliarda Sapienza, and the work of other distinguished Italian authors. He has received a National Endowment for the Arts Translation Fellowship, a Santa Maddalena Foundation Fellowship, and the PEN Grant for the English Translation of Italian Literature. His translation of the novel *Verdigris* by Michele Mari is forthcoming from And Other Stories.